End of the Line

Gideon Parry

You're a very special person. Thanks for reading my book! xx

End of the Line

Copyright © 2020 Gideon Parry

All rights reserved.

ISBN:9798653510151

The author has reserved his moral right to be identified as the author of this work.

No part of this publication may be reproduced, stored in a retrieval system, or transmitted in any form or by any means, without the permission of the copyright owner.

Disclaimer: This is a work of fiction. All names, characters, events and incidents in this book are either products of the author's imagination or are used fictitiously and any resemblance to real persons, living or dead, is purely coincidental.

End of the Line

CHAPTER ONE

As you step into the control room for shift duty, the fire door slams behind you. The supervisor doesn't look up.
'What was it *today?* Leaves on the *track?*'

You shrug your shoulders. Your attentional focus is elsewhere.

'That's a *write-up!*'

You're barely listening.

Your notion of timekeeping was determined in utero, a function of your willingness to remain in amniotic fluid until the induction of labour forced your hand.

'You've been warned *enough*, yeah?', your supervisor's saying, marking you in red. His name's Lyndon.

'Can you not *book* me today? *Please?*'

Your appeal falls on deaf ears. 'NO CAN *DO!*'

'Come on *guv*', you say.

The moniker *'guv'* feels alien to you, even after four years on the job.

'Flamin' *heck*, Peregrine, you're late every flamin' *day!*'

But you're distracted. You're currently peering out

through the rectangles of glass which frame the control room, watching a woman finger-combing a man's hair as he sits in the PHOTO-ME booth.

'Look at the *CLOCK*, it's flamin' *ATOMIC*, that clock. It loses one *second* in 100 million *years*.'

Lyndon's your least favourite supervisor. You preferred your last four supervisors. *The first one, Jason, got demoted to gate-line assistant for using premium-rate sex lines at the company's expense. The second supervisor, Bill, got demoted for long leaves of absence during which he ran an illegal construction company before Transport for London smelled a rat and parked a surveillance van outside his home.*

Your third supervisor, Tom, got relocated to an outer-lying station for making a sexual overture to a cleaner. He apparently turned round to a cleaner and said something like: 'Why don't you hoover this up, an' all?'

Your fourth supervisor, Terry, was your favourite. He was soft-spoken and had a gammy leg and used to hobble around the station or just sit at his desk reading battered paperbacks until the morning he stepped in front of a train.

Your current supervisor, Lyndon, is the fifth supervisor you've had since you started on the job. And he's currently timing you with arms akimbo as you sidle over to the charging rack, reach for the top half of a two-way radio, attach a battery block and snap it into place.

As you press TRANSMIT, there's a shudder of interference before you tame its floppy mast and slot the radio onto your utility belt.

'Platform duty!', he barks.

End of the Line

As you head to the locker rooms, which house the mess area and toilets, you pass one of your colleagues, Sidney, who walks with a slow, ponderous gait.

'Oow-right, mate? Don't worry about him… he's a bit radio', Sidney says with a smile, having watched your exchange through the control room windows.

'*Radio?*'

'Radio rental, *mental.*'

His smile is almost circular, like a crescent moon, his eyes swollen behind magnified lenses. He's wearing an ill-fitting uniform at least two sizes too big and his tie is trailing the top of his trousers, which are draped over orthopaedic shoes.

Your radio rattles, emitting a SNAPPING sound. This occurs at the fag-end of each transmission when the 'TRANSMIT' button is released.

'BASE T'ALL STAFF! USE *CORRECT* RADIO PROCEEJA. NO JOKES OR BAD LANGUAGE ON THE AIRWAVES, *YEAH?* THIS IS JUST T'*REMIND* YAZ!' SNAP!

Once inside the locker room, you head to the ceramic urinals which are partly blocked off by a stanchion and watch as steam rises from your arced discharge. There's a sign which reads NOW WASH YOUR HANDS. The word '*NOW*' has been replaced by the word '*TOMORROW*'.

The mess area is lined with lockers which stand like

End of the Line

palisades beneath an overhang of generators and humming machinery. Metallic and grey, they each have ventilation slots on their doors which resemble the gill slits on the side of sharks. Rust bubbles, clearly visible on their surfaces, display torn-out banner headlines from the sports sections of red tops.

'Gunners bottle *out!*''Is that Vierra *spitting* again? Dirty ****!' You take a seat at the mess-room table beside a notice advertising an upcoming sweepstake. On the table in front of you is a jar of *Mellow Bird's Coffee* and an abandoned mug with a picture of a daisy and the word *MARGATE* on it.

There are footsteps and a rustle. It's Buntiya the station cleaner pushing supermarket tabloids into a refuse sack in the corner of the room. He's wearing jeans with hearts sown into the legs and gold sequins on his shoes. He peers down at your jacket which, unbeknownst to you, has fallen to the floor.

'You muss pooh *dis* in your locka, *not* on di *floor!* Here is no a *disco* room, *eh?*'

'*Sorry*, Bunty!'

'SUPERVISOR TO *CHARLIE-TANGO-9*, STATE YOUR CURRENT *LOCATION!* SNAP!'

This is your call-sign. 'I'm on my way *down* to platforms, over' SNAP!

'Deed you wash di *fooball* lass nigh? Ha!..Crezy, *NOT SO?!*'

End of the Line

'I don't *know* anything about football. I know *nothing* about it, *zilch!* You *know* that, Buntiya!'

Buntiya's one of the day-shift cleaners, the majority of whom are from Ghana, Nigeria or Sierra Leone. He has cicatrix slashes on his cheeks, three raised welts denoting ritual scarification.

'*Enywey*, brodder…', he says, emitting a long, sibilant, kissing teeth sound at the sight of the littered floor.

You rise and walk towards your locker, which - you quickly notice - has been tampered with. As you open its battered door, your throat contracts with the unholy stench that rises up from it. All your belongings are caked in curry powder, your spare uniform, your pens, nothing has been spared. You remove your work jacket and pinch its collar between finger and thumb and shake violently, scattering a cloud of curry dust across the floor with Buntiya standing behind you, swinging a broom.

'Who the *hell* did this to my *LOCKER*, Buntya?'

'*Eh!* Don drop di yellow ting to di *ground!* I pick di floor all *day* for you, *not* so? Look at di *mess* you make…!'

'This isn't *my* fault!'

'My *friend!* Wus your *problem* dis manning? You have *problem* dis manning, *not* so?'

'My *problem?* Someone's attacked my *locker!* I'm being *victimised*, that's my *problem*. Lyndon will *find* the person responsible for *this*.'

Buntiya sounds a note of caution, informing you that Lyndon won't care, that's it's best if you pretended the incident had never happened.

'Why's *that*, Bunty?'

'*Eh?* Don you *know* dis?'

'Don't I know *what?* Tell me, *Bunty!*'

He shakes his head as if he knows more than he's willing to let on, as if there's a conspiracy of silence he's been sworn to, as if you have some sort of pariah status on the station. He continues sweeping with forceful thrusts of his broom, thumping it into corners and grunting with each successive motion. He's now weaving a mop from side to side with single-minded focus.

Leaning into your locker, you whip out your high-vi tabard, hold it at arm's length and shake it as Buntiya mops the floor with rhythmic slaps behind you.

'*Hey!* Don *do* dis! Dis is an *eatin'* room! It mustn't bi *darty*, it muss be *clean!*'

You look at Buntya with an apologetic shrug as you rub the roundel on the front of your cap to a glistening burnish, then wash your hands. The water bounces off your upturned fingers in sheets of diaphanous yellow.

There's a sudden *'thunk!'* as Lyndon goose steps into the room, the door slamming behind him.

End of the Line

'WHAT CHEW *DOIN'*'ERE?'

'Getting *changed*, guv'

'You's SUPPOSTA BE ON THEM *PLATFORMS!*', he carps. Lyndon has distinctive features. His forehead is a patchwork of intersecting lines and his eyes are a little too close-set. He suffers from *small man's* disease, a Napoleonic complex born of a feeling of inadequacy about his height, or lack thereof. He stands at 5 foot and has a limp and a lampshade moustache that quivers at the slightest provocation. It's quivering now.

'My locker's been VANDALISED. Someone's broken into it and thrown CURRY powder *everywhere*, all over my UNIFORM. My locker's been *vandalised*, guv!'

'I don't *care* what's 'BIN' *what*, Peregrine! GET DOWN THEM PLATFORMS!....*NOW!*'

Buntiya twists the mop into the wringer, looks up, shoots you a glance that says *'I told you so'* and continues to attack the floor.

In 5 minutes, probably less, you'll have descended into the Dantean depths, the Dantean bowels of the earth where you'll be subjugated to the thankless task of being a visible presence on the platforms. Visible yet oddly invisible, merging into the surrounding background, with Lyndon monitoring you like a Red-tailed hawk.

You brazenly hop onto the escalator despite the faint whiff of turmeric wafting from you and, vectoring downwards, hop off the escalator, walk through a cross-passageway and over a humped walkway towards the platforms, passing a wall-mounted journey planner which looks like an electrical circuit diagram. Across the station marked *VICTORIA*, someone's scribbled *POSH SPICE*. As you walk past condensers, access panels, belly-curved vending machines and first-aid lockers, you notice all the graffiti.

'QPR MOB score against *West Ham!'*

Then a radio message. 'A little *parcel* comin' up *your* way!' SNAP!

It's your colleague, Big Pete, notifying the gate-line staff of an attractive woman making her way up from platform to street level. Big Pete cuts an intimidating figure. He's almost as wide as he is tall, with one eye higher than the other, like in a Picasso portrait. His cheeks are crosshatched with stubble and he has a French crop haircut and a stud in both earlobes. You imagine he's smiling right now, his lips pressed against the microphone indentations, ready to deliver a glib comment.

'A *parcel?*' SNAP!

'A 6-foot *package*' SNAP!

'Supervisor to *Echo-1*, PETE, stop *cloggin'* them *airways*, yeah?… Check the right posters are in the right *frames* or summink, *yeah?*' SNAP!

'Pete, just *clocked* it. Legs up to the *sky*…' SNAP!

End of the Line

'Get yer *gums* round me *plums!*...' SNAP!

You pass a row of shiny decals warning passengers of gaps, drops, death and electrocution. Someone's scribbled *'I LUV YOU'* across Jennifer Lopez's posterior on a poster for an upcoming movie, which has been defaced with bubble-gum snot-balls plugged into her nostrils.

You see Hobo Jack. He seems to have become slightly more crazed than the last time you saw him. An old, skinny guy with a philosopher's beard and eyes like cigarette ash, he walks with the aid of a pike staff and carries a placard, a corrugated thing zipped into the back of his rucksack. It reads: *'HOBO JACK-USA, EUROPE, MID EAST'.*

You walk on and notice some effluent dripping into a cup, and from the cup into a bag, and from the bag into a bucket, above which hangs a hot deal Mastercard ad, promising the holiday of a lifetime in some island paradise.

Further along are posters depicting various celebrity-endorsed products featuring *Dolce & Gabbana* models, their arms akimbo, their freckled faces and angular jawlines beckoning you into their glamorous worlds. Across one of the model's foreheads someone's scribbled:

COKE PROBLEM.

Your radio throbs at your hip. 'Base to all *radios*. This is a combine-wide message. There's a g'tleman, about fifty and balding, brown overcoat and jeans.

End of the Line

He's left a suicide note on his breakfast table. Keep your eyes *peeled*, he could be *anywhere* on the combine, over and *out*.' SNAP!

You see a light-box poster advertising *DADDY BURGERS* and a hoarding for the musical Singing in the rain. Someone's crossed out the last four letters in the word *'singing'* and appended two cartoon stick-figures copulating beneath an umbrella. The altered strapline reads: *Sin in the rain*.

As you patrol the platforms, your mind wanders back to your first week on the job.

You had a colleague, an old Irishman who went by the name of Eamon who was rostered at Goodge Street, the first station you worked at. The group station manager had stood him down from duties pending disciplinary action.

Eamon used to make involuntary noises and smelt like rotten potatoes. He used to pace about and couldn't keep still even for a moment. If he was sitting, his leg would jerk or his arm would twitch and he would chain drink cups of tea. He told you that he'd been stood down because he'd come to work in half a uniform, but you knew better. You were privy to the real reason he's been relieved of his duties, pending disciplinary action. His station assistant colleagues, referred to at the time as LDRs, had lodged a complaint and refused to work with him on account of his throat-choking odour. He always wore the same mac and cardigan under his nylon work jacket, a mac and cardigan he'd probably never washed.

The truth was, Eamon had been disciplined for refusing to obey a supervisory injunction to go home and clean his clothes. You wondered why they didn't just place him on

End of the Line

compassionate leave, indefinitely.

His hair was white with a patch of yellow on top, his face ruddy, his eyes fixed with a hawk-like stare, but his eyes were really dead, they were like two little coat buttons attached to his face.

On one occasion, you watched him eating a McMuffin breakfast, which he proceeded to wolf down by spilling egg and bacon down his chin. And you recall the caked snot dangling from his nostrils and the white beads of dried spittle at the corners of his mouth as he sat with his legs twitching like an upended cockroach in its final death throes.

Beside him on the floor of the messroom table, Eamon had a plaid laundry bag filled with tea bags and digestive biscuits. When he moved his lips to speak, his voice quivered and his words made no sense. An abiding memory you have of him was during the run-up to Christmas. It was a couple of days before Christmas Eve that he arrived in a taxi to facilitate the transport of groceries which he proceeded to empty onto the kitchen counter. He wanted to surprise his colleagues with a festive meal, but no one would touch what he'd spent hours preparing. His colleagues gave the kitchen a wide berth, leaving him to eat alone, surrounded by pots, pans and the stench of unwashed skin.

Eamon had been on the job since 1971 and had begun his slow descent into madness over many years. Away from work, he'd walk around in uniform. Once, en route to Lourdes as a pilgrim, he wore his station uniform, including his peaked cap, and people – for some reason - mistook him for a postman.

He never spent money on anything except sweet-meal biscuits and Typhoo tea, and kept all his unopened wage packets

End of the Line

under his bedroom mattress.

A few months after his disciplinary hearing, he was discovered dead, his bedsit filled with half-drunk cups of tea and digestive biscuits and 70,000 pounds in cash hidden beneath his mattress.

A passenger interrupts your animatronic pacing.

'Er…are you *staff* here?'

'Yes…'

'I *see*. Where's the way *out?*'

You point to the brightly-lit, illuminated sign which says: 'WAY OUT'.

Another passenger, carrying a *JADE* sport-bag stops you, looking distractedly at his watch.

'*Excuse* me mate, how *long's* the next *train?*'

'About 108 metres, front to back.'

'No, I *meant* how long a *wait* is it until the next train comes *in?*'

'*Oh*', you say innocently, squinting up at the countdown board which displays the minutes in illuminated, dot-matrix lettering.

'4 *minutes*, mate.'

A woman approaches and asks for the time. You point to the giant, unmissably positioned digital clock on the tunnel headwall. She nods, thanks you.

'How do I get to High Street *Ken?*'

End of the Line

'Stay on *this* platform.'

'Do I need to *change?*'

'No, you look fine as you *are*.'

'*No*, I meant do I need to change *trains?*'

'No. Stay on *this* platform.'

'And how to I *know* which way the *train's* coming *in?*'

'See the *traffic* lights on the *headwall?*'

'Yes.'

'It won't be coming in from *that* end.'

'I *see*, thanks.'

'By the *way*, your handbag's open. Pickpockets will happily attempt to abstract your *purse*, madam.'

'Oh, *thanks*.'

'*Excuse* mate!'

'*Yes?*'

'What time are the *rides?*'

'*What* rides?'

'Them *donkey* rides.'

'*What* donkey rides?'

'Them donkey rides on Blackpool *beach*.'

'But we're in *London*.'

End of the Line

'I thought you was, like, *information*, mate?'

In the distance, you see the regular with the pram. Sandra, the lipstick lesbian with the intense blue eyes.

You say hi and she smiles back at you and, as always, you help her up from platform level with her buggy. If she were an elderly lady with a prolapse herniation, you might explain that it wasn't your job to be a station porter, that you're not insured to heft people's luggage up and down. But when you harbour a secret crush, you make exceptions.

'How's your bundle of *joy* today, Sandra?'

'Oh, Daisy's doing quite well, *aren't* we Daisy?'

'Mummy, what's that smell?'

'I think that's *me*, Daisy. I was cooking *curry* earlier', you say, sniffing your collar. 'I must have got carried away with the *turmeric*.'

'Oh, nice, what *sort* of curry *was* it?', Sandra asks.

'Oh…just your *standard*.'

You heft Sandra's strapped-in toddler up the fixed stairway as you continue to ask *faux*-concerned questions about Daisy. Sandra responds with perfunctory phrases and fake chuckles, since you're the only station assistant who ever helps her.

'Easy…*there* we go', you say, setting down the wheels of the pram. 'And be a good *girl* to mummy, Daisy', you add, waving goodbye to mother and child and

End of the Line

heading back down to the platforms, somewhat out of breath.

The radio vibrates at your hip.

'Big Pete t'base!' SNAP!

'Pass your *MASSAGE*, over…and use your designated *call* sign next time, Pete, *yeah?*' SNAP!

Lyndon likes to say *'MASSAGE'* instead of *'MESSAGE'* with a self-satisfied smile on his lips. He's particularly fond of saying it with a drawn-out stress on its second syllable.

'There's a *defect* on the track, guv, and I wanna *report* it, *over.*' SNAP!

'*You* standing there, YOU'RE the defect.' SNAP!

'It looks like a *track* wedge has fallen out, or *summink*, guv.' SNAP!

'How *many?* You got a *visual* on it?' SNAP!

'One. Lying on its side. *Loose.*' SNAP!

'Base received.' SNAP!

'S'long as it's not half a *dozen* loose wedges we're alright, ain't we, guv?' SNAP!

'S'long as YOU keep *away* from it, we're alright.' SNAP!

'By the *way*, Pete, that despatch come and *go* yet, over?'

'Not *yet* guv…'

End of the Line

'Bit *late*, ain't he?'

'Must've used Peregrine's *alarm* this morning.' SNAP!

'Have you checked them *frames*, Pete?'

'I got cut *off* there. What wos *that?*..summink about *flames?*'

'No, *frames!*'

'These radios are about t'give up the *ghost*, like.'

'Pete, *do* us a favour. Could ya check the state of them *poster* frames an' *that?* I *did* ask ya before, but you was obviously too *busy* doing sod *all.*'

'I *forgot* about them *frames*, guv. Must've been *side*-tracked…*ha-ha!* That was a *joke*…*SIDE*-TRACKED, *get* it?'

'Go and check them *frames* then Pete, *yeah?* Let us know if anyfink is *floppin'* or *danglin'*, yeah?'

'Only me *tackle.*'

'*Whassat?*'

'I didn't say *nuffink.*'

'Keep it *clean* Pete, *yeah?* And 'ave a bit of a *nose* around, check the platforms for *slip* hazards an' that, *over.*'

'That's a *10-4*, over.'

A different voice cuts in. It's Del, trivia geek Del, a station assistant with a mooncalf face, jam-jar

End of the Line

glasses and a head like a watermelon.

'*Del* 'ere. Starter for *10*. Who sang *'Misty Blue'?*' SNAP!

'*Madonna?*'

'You's 'aving a *laugh*, inch ya?' SNAP!

'No, *honest*. I fought it *was* Madonna.' SNAP!

'*Okay*, give you's lot a *clue*. Soul. Black. Female…' SNAP!

'Dorothy *Moore?*' SNAP!

'Spot *on!*' SNAP!

'Is she related to *Roger* or *Patrick?*' SNAP!

'How about *'Ma cheri amour?'* Who sang *that?*'

'Weren't that the *blind* geeza, the *black* one?' SNAP!

'Stevie Wonder, *yeah*, well *done!* How about *'The harder they fall, the harder they come'?*'

'You *sure* that's *right?*'

'I *meant*, the other way *round!* 'SNAP!

'The harder they *come*, then?'

'*Thas* the one'. SNAP!

'Jimmy *Cliff?*'

'Spot *on!*'

'BASE TO ALL RADIOS, KEEP THE AIRWAVES CLEAR. YOUR RADIOS AREN'T

FER the ol' hit parade an' that, yeah?!'SNAP!

'What-bout *'Good morning Sunshine?'*

'*Donovan.*' SNAP!

'*Na*...Alex *Day*. Here's a *harder* one: *'The day that curly Billy shot down crazy Sam McGee'?'*

'*Dunno!*'

'It was the *Hollies*' SNAP!

'SUPERVISOR TO ALL STAFF, *STOPPIT* NOW, *YEAH?* WHAT IF SOMEONE'S TRYIN' T'*CONTACT* ME? KEEP THEM WAVES *CLEAR*, YEAH?...Actually, as it *happens*, I *do* have an important message for *you's* lot. A message from the *British Transport Police*. Some vagrant. Old, skinny, wearing a long, grey *mac*. He's somewhere on the combine, walking up and down escalators, standing up close behind skirted women. He has little mirrors on his toecaps. *BTP* say he's a repeat offender, over and *out.*' SNAP!

'Message *received* and *understood*, over' SNAP!

You continue to patrol in the ferrety light, kicking a mound of papers beneath your feet which quiver as a soot-encrusted mouse appears, glances around furtively, twitches its nose, then darts across the platform and into the darkness beneath the ballast. You lean over and pick up what looks like a postcard from the pile of papers. It reads:

'Dear Barbara, the dreary weather of a traditional English winter is probably not what most people would consider a

End of the Line

good introduction to a new country'.

You throw the postcard back on the platform floor and walk over to the belly-curved vending machine, across which someone's scribbled: *'DO NOT WASTE YOUR MONEY ON THIS DISHONEST, DISHONOURABLE GADGET!!!'* You soon discover why. Someone's lodged a coin beneath the money tray to obstruct its change-release mechanism. You work the coin loose until a small mountain of cash clatters into the change-dish. You quickly scoop it up.

You walk on now, past a poster depicting a semi-clad go-go dancer across which someone's appended the words *'LESBIAN AVENGERS'.*

'Base to Sierra 5, Del, *do* us a favour, make a P.A. announcement about the delays on the *Pic*, over?'

'Wos the *reason* guv?'

'DUNNO! JUST MAKE *UP* A REASON, *yeah?*'

You're given permission to surface now, for a spot of gate-line duty before your shift wraps up. You can't wait to be *free*, to be released into the *light*.

End of the Line

CHAPTER TWO

The art school graduation season has begun. You buy a copy of *Time Out magazine* and check the relevant dates so you can attend some private views. It seems like the perfect way to meet a potential arty girlfriend, which is your long-held ambition.

It's a few days later and you're heading to the opening at one of London's hippest, big name art schools. Having just ingested some *Xanax,* you feel super-relaxed as you stride past the security goons and enter the hallowed entrance hall of the art school building.

There are a lot of intelligent-looking, beautifully-dressed women tonight, but you're unsure of how to break the ice with any of them. You approach a cultivated-looking woman in figure-hugging jeans and then espy an even more beguiling lady with flaxen locks and decide to forgo the *first* woman for the *second*. Then you lose sight of the *second* woman and see the *first* again.

But it's difficult to find the right words to ignite a conversation in order to see who you *gel* with, plus, there are too many impenetrable cliques, too much perceived competition from chiselled-featured guys wearing *Faiosa* framed glasses and designer stubble or midnight-blue denim and *Ralph Lauren* caps worn at strategic angles. The place is aswarm with people wearing python skin loafers and *Tiger* lace-ups and *Barbour* jackets with silk scarves and fedora hats.

End of the Line

As you walk towards the main body of the exhibition, you wonder what your tube colleagues would make of the art you're about to be confronted by.

'Join the *conflab*, Crispin!' you overhear someone saying to a guy wearing winkle pickers and a cap cocked strategically to one side. People are confabulating in cliques on the concrete mounds surrounding the main entranceway and all the way out to the campus lawns.

You walk around, taking in the raft of work ranged across five floors of cubicled space. It's complete visual *overload*. There are paint-splattered photos and time-line pieces and a pile of wood pigeons emitting exotic birdcalls and the scrotum of a buffalo rendered in ebonized wood entitled *BUTCHER'S LARDER* and a video of two entwined shadows, titled *'SOFT VALUES AND HARD VEINS'*.

You enter an artist's space via a flimsy curtain. Immediately, you're confronted by shelves heaving with canopic jars, oracle boxes, preserved *'aliens'*, a reliquary of a broken heart, a crucified spider, an insect in amber, a whelked snail pressed beneath a tortoise, the skeletal remains of a *puffa* fish, an autopsied *urchin*, a jar marked *TISSUE SAMPLE OF A DOLL* and a set of false teeth submerged within a tumbler.

Wandering deeper into this Aladdin's cave of a room you notice a gurney-like table with straps attached to it and a bookcase with a leather-bound copy of the *HOLY BIBLE* leaning against a copy of

End of the Line

120 DAYS OF SODOM.

You pick up some complementary wine, exit the space and round a corner. Confronting you now is a twin installation comprising a diorama of Trafalgar Square in miniature. The title of the first installation is *NELSON'S COLUMN*. In it admiral Lord nelson has a protrusion in the groin vicinity of his naval tunic as his stands before the nation with one foot lodged dramatically forward.

The sister piece to *NELSON'S COLUMN* comprises a mock-up of Nelson wearing his bicorn hat, now replaced by a giant pigeon perched high above Trafalgar Square and flanked by two falcons, two bay-winged hawks and four bronze raptors down below, which have replaced the traditional bronze lions at the column's base. To the east of the esplanade in the area of St Martin-in-the-Fields, Lord Nelson stands proudly upon the forth plinth, dwarfed by the giant pigeon looming high above, its wings frozen in mid-flap. This sister piece, according to its nearby caption, is titled *PIGEON SQUARE*.

You notice a woman nearby, dressed in jeans which are tucked into boots lined with pancake heels. You attempt a stab at conversation.

'Are these *your* pieces?', you ask.

'Yes.'

'They're very *evocative*'

Evocative is a great adjective to use in these arty environments, as is *pared down* and *impactful*.

End of the Line

'*Thanks*', she says.

'Could you tell me about the ideas that have *informed* your *practice*, and about the *genesis* of your pieces?'

Words like *practice*, *genesis* and *inform* are also good words to use at private views and show that you're not a *philistine*, even if you *are*.

'I'd *prefer* it if you simply responded to my work as you see *fit*', she says. 'I'm disinclined to *discuss* it.'

'Well, they're very *nuanced*, I must say.'

Nuanced is another good word to throw in there.

'Well, *look*…okay', she begins reluctantly, 'With regard to the installation on the *left*, *NELSON'S COLUMN*, well, Nelson was a national *war* hero. But as you must *surely* know, combat has traditionally been the exclusive domain of the *masculine*. My work addresses the inherent phallocentric nature of military conflict.'

'That's *super* interesting. How about your *sister* piece?'

'PIGEON SQUARE? *Gosh!* If you *really* want to discuss heroism, pigeons have been *far* more heroic than humans *ever* have been. They ought to be *commemorated* rather than being *consigned* to the dust-heap of *history*. Ever heard of *G I Joe* the *pigeon*?'

'No.'

'Well, G I Joe was quite a *remarkable* pigeon who, with single-winged determination, saved the lives of

End of the Line

1000 allied troops during World War 2. Pigeons were used during *both* world wars to convey messages across enemy lines. Did you *know* that?'

'I *didn't*. What about the *raptors?* Why have you replaced the *lions* with *raptors?*"

'I'll *tell* you *why!* Because Ken Livingstone - in his infinite *wisdom* - decided to rid Trafalgar square of its feral pigeons, that's *why!*'

'I didn't *know* that…I see. *Interesting.*'

'*Didn't* you? Well, there's a by-law that states you can be *fined* for feeding pigeons in the square now. All the seed sellers have been forced *out* of the esplanade and the authorities are now scaring pigeons *away* through the employment of aggressive *means*. They use falconers armed with *raptors* and *megaphones* to scare them *off*. Pigeons have been deemed *pests* and I was under the impression we were a nation of *animal*-lovers!'

'I actually *like* pigeons, I think they get a bad *rap*.'

'You *like* them?'

'I think they're *great*, yes.'

'Okay, well, that's *good*.'

'I think they're really *cute* and kind of *feathery*. By the way, what does the acronym *'C.U.N.T'* in your installation *'PIGEON SQUARE'* stand for?'

'Oh, *that?* It stands for Nelson's four major battles – Copenhagen, Utrecht, the Nile and Trafalgar.'

End of the Line

'I *see*. And what's your *name*, by the way?'

'*Marcella*…', she says, extending her hand.

'Pleased to *meet* you, Marcella.'

'And you *are?*'

'Peregrine.'

'Oh *dear*…!'

'What's *wrong?*'

'It's not my favourite name, I'm really *sorry*, it's not *your* fault, of course, but it carries negative *connotations* for me.'

'Why's *that?*'

'Because the *Peregrine Falcon* is the natural *enemy* of the pigeon. During a hunting stoop, they swoop down and *rip* these poor pigeons to *death*.'

'*Tell* me something, Marcella. The pigeons in Trafalgar Square, or the ones that at least *used* to be in Trafalgar Square were *feral*, but the ones that were used in the *war* effort *weren't*. Am I *right?*'

'And your *point* being?'

'Well, *nothing* really, just an observation. Anyway, great work, Marcella, keep it *up!* I hope *Nelson* does *too*.'

'That's quite a *puerile* comment!'

'A *joke*, Marcella. Anyway…lovely *meeting* you.'

End of the Line

Pigeons! They're *rats* with *wings* you think to yourself as you continue to orbit the exhibition. You approach an internally-lit cabinet containing a single bottle of detergent set high on a cardboard plinth around which are gathered a group of people, passing comment. You listen in. A man wearing a floral cravat and a gaberdine jacket is holding court. 'This bottle was once purely *utilitarian*, but its Duchampian *de-worlding* from the everyday to the *vicinage* - if you will - of the gallery space has turned it into something frightfully *eroticised*, wouldn't you *say*, Cassandra?'

'Yes, I *would*. The last piece we saw was rather *beastly*, but *this* piece, with its curvilinear *dips* and *bulges* is visually *arresting*, Sebastian. Very Duchampian, *too*.'

An elderly woman, balancing on a wooden cane, leans in conspiratorially. 'Whatever will they think of next, these people! This art thingamyboby is a con, if you ask me!'

You watch Sebastian as he studies the elderly lady before venturing a considered response. 'It is dangerous to venture *generalisations*, madam, if I *may* be so bold. Could I ask your *name?*'

'It's *Gladys*.'

'Gladys, this is certainly *not* an art con. For *one* thing, the negation of the object's inherent *functionality* via the process of re-contextualisation *creates* art, as evidenced by the artist being strategically *engaged* within the conceptual framework of the

End of the Line

Duchampian tradition. I *mean*, Gladys, are you more strengthened now in the conviction that I might be *right?*'

Gladys, after a second or two of wide-eyed befuddlement, slides the spectacles off the end of her nose and raises the crook handle of her cane. 'Why aren't there any pictures of *puppies* or *horses* in this exhibition?'

Sebastian studies her for a moment. 'Sentimental *kitsch*, madam, unless made with ironic knowing, *isn't* art, it's bad *decoration*.'

You consider Sebastian and Cassandra's earlier conversational exchange for a moment. Duchamp was the artist who, in 1917, presented a found object - a urinal - with the name *'R. Mutt'* signed across it, claiming later that *'choice is equal to creation'*. As you mull over the notion of the readymade, you notice that Sebastian has turned back to the group, his arms gesticulating in the air.

'I see this piece as a comment on the notion of commodity fetishism, that whole *Marxist* thing…'

'*Indeed*, Sebastian. Moreover, I see this bottle as being quite *phallic*, myself.'

'Oh *Cassandra*, to me bottles are *RARELY* phallic…'

It takes a second for the penny to drop, but what Sebastian has actually just said is that bottles are *REALLY* phallic. It just sounded like *RARELY*, because of his plummy accent.

End of the Line

You walk on, following the 'MORE ART *THIS WAY*' signs and pass a sculpture of Gordon Ramsey in a heightened state of arousal, titled *THE RISE OF THE CELEBRITY CHEF*.

You see the old woman again. She's squinting at an explanatory wall text in confusion.

'Enjoying the *show*, Gladys?', you ask.

'*No*, dear…I'm *not*.'

'Why *not*, Gladys?'

'Why aren't there any cheery *waterfalls* or pretty pictures of *kittens* and all that?'

'That would be *nice*, I suppose, *wouldn't* it, Gladys?'

'I don't *understand* this explanation, *deary*. Says here: 'This work exists in the space between *uncertainty* and *assurance*'. Well, I'm more flummoxed *now* than I blinking was 2 *minutes* ago, before I *read* it. In *my* day, son, people used to say what they *meant*. I dunno, I think it all went wrong with that fella who cut his *ear* off.'

'Fair *point*', you say, walking on.

As you round a corner, you find yourself face-to-face with something that gives you a visceral punch. *'Visceral'* is another great word to use in an environment like this one. Standing before you now is a life-size sculpture of a gorilla which has been disembowelled by a ceremonial sword and, as if this wasn't enough, it has an axe through its skull and a screwdriver through its arm. A visceral *punch*, if ever there was one.

'This monkey's got a bit of a *problem*', someone says, inspecting the sculpture through a pair of Wayfarers.

You walk on, passing a sculpture of two gnomes standing balefully beside each other, titled *GNOME STEALING A GNOME FROM ANOTHER GNOME'S GARDEN*, then past a coconut waterfall and a dog wearing a loup and an egg machine made from yarn and a floor-based puddle of grease. You walk on. 'I believe we met last year at that soiree in *Saltzberg,*', says a man in wingtip brogues to a woman wearing cork wedges. You espy an interesting-looking arty woman sipping from an *Asaki Black*. You stop shyly and posit a question. 'What do you think of the work this year?' She smiles, shrugs. 'Not *much* really. How about *you?* Are you *exposing* yourself here tonight?'

'What do you *mean?*' 'I mean, you have zum *verk* in zis *exposition?*'

'Ah, not *this* year. I've already *been* to art school.'

'Ah. Zis is *nice*.'

'So, what do you think of the *show* this year?'

'Zis is *bullshit*, ja?'

'What, the whole *show?*'

'Some of ziz is sehr *funny*, sehr lustig, *nein?*'

As you consider what to say next, a man wearing a

End of the Line

dress shirt, pleated slacks and penny loafers appears out of nowhere, glances at you and reclaims the woman by the arm, steering her away to safety, as if you somehow posed some mortal danger. You continue walking, past a prototype of a wind-powered record-player on wheels and a drawing of the Millennium wheel being cycled by a recumbent woman with webbed feet. Then past a painting of Batman and Robin behind a bicycle shed, locked in carnal embrace. You notice a giant egg slicer made of marble and a cast of two tortoises, their necks entwined, titled *TANTRIC STORM*. Nearby is a bank of television screens nestled together in a seemingly arbitrary pile, each depicting the same looped image: A person in flames at various stages of immolation, set to Beethoven's Ninth symphony.

You stop briefly to admire a painting of a person looking at a painting, looking at a painting.

You see a friendly, cultured-looking woman standing alone nursing a drink and watch as she shifts her weight from one glass-healed shoe to the other. She appears to be protecting a group of paintings.

'*Hi* there, just wondering if you're the exhibiting *artist*.'

'I am, *yes*', she smiles.

'Interesting work, what's your work *about?*'

'It's about making the invisible *visible* and the visible *invisible*.'

'That's *super* interesting. What's the *inspiration* behind

End of the Line

your practice?'

'Anthroposophy and biomorphic forms. I use them to reference Martian script and the cosmic *narrative*.'

'That's *super* fascinating. You don't seem to have compromised the *energy* of the piece, or made *concessions*.'

'Thanks, I try *not* to. I'm very interested in the dualism between *matter* and *spirit*, but I think that's quite *obvious*, if you really care to *engage* with the work.'

'And what about *that* painting, the one to the *left* of it?'

'That one's to do with ectoplasmic nimbuses.'

You nod, considering it for a moment, then chat to her some more until you sense some mutual chemistry.

'Do you, *perhaps*, want to go out for a *drink* sometime?', you ask, casually.

Silence.

'Can you at least give me, like, a *sign?*', you smile.

'My silence *is* your sign.'

You stare down at your shoes, look up.

'Oh, *hi* Edward!', she says, refocussing her attention, now conversing with a man wearing a Ralph Lauren bike jacket, Armani slim fits and tasselled loafers. Feeling awkward, you walk on, round a corner and gaze up at the first thing you see, which is a trumpet-blowing amoretto perched on a low stump and fashioned from *'no need to sift'* McDougal's flour.

Soon you come across a large video screen depicting a shaky camera journey through a tube station titled *OSMOTIC BODY*. This is too close for comfort, you've come out tonight in part to *forget* about the day job which gnaws at your soul, and against which art is the perfect counterweight. Art, in your opinion, possesses the power to *feed* the soul, to *heal* it, to *replenish* it You take a deep breath and walk on, past three supermarket trolleys adorned with mutant growths and limp, desiccated carrots.

Opposite you now, is an installation titled *JAM TARTS* which features two street walkers, fashioned from pastry and jam. Nearby, there's an installation of cardboard boxes piled beneath a ceiling of string, titled *SKULL IN THE DESERT*.

You notice a man with a green face and a red cigarette, an ashen excrescence protruding from his neck, titled *THE DECONSTRUCTION OF IDENTITY* beside two wobbling new-borns, one in red, the other in orange, both shiny and gelatinous, titled *JELLY BABIES*, which is adjacent to a hungry-looking apex predator imprisoned within a tank of formaldehyde.

You pick up some complementary Cranberry juice and glance round at some ceiling and sound installations and then watch a buzzing video projection beside a notice which reads:

End of the Line

'Due to British obscenity laws, I can't show my video piece to the public, since it contains the uncovered image of an *erect* penis'.

You wonder all of a sudden why you've seen so many intimate images of every conceivable part of the female anatomy, yet an *erect* penis is still considered *verboten.*

You briefly join a small circle of people who are watching a live performance of a woman dressed as a vacuum cleaner who's gliding backwards and forwards and decide to walk up to the next level to see the remainder of the show.

'That piece is *fiendishly* good. It radiates a sort of *nebulous* energy. Here's to art! *Chairs!*'

'Yes, *indeed!* Here's to *art!* Cheers!'

As you round the next corner, you come face to face with a row of near-empty CAVA'S, a can of MILLER LITE and three bottles of LEFFE sitting idly on a shelf and wonder, for a moment, whether this is an installation or just a collection of semi-abandoned beer bottles.

There's a crowd encircling a projection of somebody sitting on a stool, getting up from the stool and sitting back down on it again. This is on a continuous loop and it's captivating a handful of random onlookers.

You pause here and there to peruse rectangles of duck-foot quotes detailing artistic intentions. 'There's a lot more *sex* in the show this year',

End of the Line

someone says, which is a comment you hear *every* year.

You enter someone's sanctified alcove, boxed within whitened partitions and hover for a while.

'So, what is your piece *about?*', you ask the artist, who's wearing a pair of Wayfarers, Thai fishermans's slacks and Havaiana flip-flops.

'Do you *really* want to know?', she says.

'Sure, I'm *curious*.'

'Grab a *seat* and I'll *tell* you. Sit on that padded armchair over *there*.'

'*Ah!* To sit down and let the blood *settle* is such welcome *relief*.'

'Don't you enjoy walking around art shows? You make it sound like it's a *tiresome* undertaking.'

'Oh, yes, of *course* I do, and *no*, it *isn't*. So, what's your work *about?*'

'My work systematically refutes the dogmatism of the *so-called* grand narratives and dismantles the means by which they've achieved legitimation.'

'*Super* interesting. And, what are your *interests*, besides making *art?*'

End of the Line

'Do you mind if we stick to discussing my *work?*'

'Sure, no *problem.*'

'Any thoughts regarding what you *see?* In my *work*, I mean?'

'There's a very apparent conjuration between idea and execution.'

'Are you *drunk?*' she responds. 'That's a rather *pretentious* thing to say. I guess the red wine is pretty *lethal* this year! *Wait*, isn't that *cranberry* juice?'

'Maybe, I'm not *sure*. So, when do you finish *finish?*' you ask, changing the subject.

'End of *July.*'

You now rise nodding from the padded armchair. You've clearly made a great impression, but only on the seat you've just vacated. Your gauche conversational stabs have, thus far, fallen flat this evening.

You wander over to the makeshift bar. As you approach the bar, the bar tender tells you that the free booze has run dry, so you buy a beer and look at a photo of a mother and a baby in a tattoo parlour. The baby is having its forearm tattooed with the word *'MUM'*, beside which is a thematically similar piece depicting a force-feeding baby machine which is inlaid with a row of seats, each attached to an anti-colic rubber nipple.

You follow the 'EXHIBITION CONTINUES' sign one final time, passing a video of a motorbike wending its way through a cage of concrete kettles

End of the Line

and past a fake tree fashioned from wood and standing at an improbable angle, its scalloped limbs wrapped chrysalis-like in cling-film.

'You have a wonderful *sensibility*…', you say to the exhibiting artist.

'Oh, *thanks!* My work is about manufacturing tensions through *happenstance*. I think the tree's extemporaneousness lends it a sense of *ambivalence*, don't you *think?*'

'I can really see that, yes.'

'You know, I always try to *challenge* the viewer into entering a strategic *dialogue* with my pieces.'

'Oh, *absolutely*, quite.'

'My intention for the piece was to interrogate the nature of *nature*, the nature of nature *itself*, although the meaning isn't fixed, it's open-*ended*…'

'Pretty interesting stuff, I *must* say.'

'Well, it was nice talking to you, but I've got to mingle. What did you say your name was?'

'I didn't, it's Peregrine. I was just about to leave, actually.

'And what do you do, Peregrine?'

'Me? Oh, I work in the travel industry.'

CHAPTER THREE

It's the following morning and you're on your way to work, on a train which is idling between stations.

'This is your driver speaking. I apologise for the lack of forward movement.'

A few seconds pass in silence, broken only by the rustling of newspapers and some sporadic throat-clearing.

'Apologises *again* for the delay, but the driver for this train is on the train *behind* this train…'

Another 4 minutes pass.

'Ladies and gents, I'm afraid there's now *signal* failure. I'll keep you *posted*.'

3 minutes later.

'*Sorry* to inform you of *this*, but the signal failure's now turned into a broken *rail*…I'm trying to contact the controller, but communications have basically *had* it.'

5 minutes later. 'Ladies and gents, radio communication has now been partially restored. Bad news I'm *afraid*, they've now imposed a 5 mile an hour *speed* restriction.'

2 minutes later.

There's a shudder. The carriage lights flicker. Some forward movement, then a sharp application of brakes. The driver comes back on the P.A. 'Latest update. The train is being *withdrawn* from service and terminating at the next station.'

End of the Line

6 minutes later you exit the station. You're late.

A wino walks up to you. 'DRINK!', he says, 'IS MY *LIFE* SQUIRE!'

'Oy mate! *Psst!* 'Ere! You wanna hands-*free?*', says someone else.

'No, thanks.'

'How about some spare change then, pal?'

'*Excuse* me sir', someone in a suit says. You raise your eyebrows. '*Sir*, do you believe in *Jesus?*'

You shrug your shoulders, continue walking.

'Sir! Hello, *sir!* If you live without *Jesus*, you're a *sheep* without a *shepherd!*...Sir!....*Sir?*'

You soon arrive at a nearby bus stop. 'Last night's supper or this morning's breakfast?' someone says, looking at a pigeon that's moving with little jerks of the head and pecking at some scraps. You forgo the bus idea and walk. It's probably quicker. Tacked to a tree you pass in the rain, a sign reads:

'CAN YOU HELP FIND MY BUGGIE? GREY, CALL'D BILLY. HE'S A GOOD TALKER. I CAN OFFER A RWARD. HE'S GREY-HAIRED, OVERWEIGHT. HAD THE *SNIP*, TOO.'

End of the Line

The building looming large on the horizon ahead of you is your rostered station. A ticket tout intercepts you as you negotiate the steps.

'Psst! Need a *ticket* boss?'

'I'm *okay*.'

'Mate! All *right?*... *Need* something? Pills? *Ecstasy?*...It's *mint*. Quality. It'll get ya *buzzing*, mate. *Guaranteed*. Want some *ganja?* Come 'ere and 'ave a *sniff*, smell the *lavender*, mate.'

You shake your head, no.

'How's about helpin' me out with twenty *pence*, then, pal?'

As you jog through the lattice gates, you can see that Lyndon already has his red pen in the air. He doesn't look up. You make an appeal to reason.

'Problems on the *tube*', you say, breathless. 'You can *fact* check it, if you want.'

'No can *do!*'

'This is *not* some feeble excuse, there were *legit* delays this morning, guv.'

'I'M *BOOKING* YA. 50 *MINUTES*.'

You pass Sidney on the barriers.

'*Out* last night, was *ya?*'

'I went to a private view.'

'Zat a *peep* show or summink?'

End of the Line

'It's an *art* thing.'

You head down one of the escalators, the second of which is hung with the sign 'OUT OF COMISSION'. A man sets his briefcase down with an audible thud.

'Can you *fix* these damn *escalators?*'

'I'm *not* an escalator engineer, sorry.'

'YOU *KNOW* WHAT I DAMN *MEAN!*'

At the escalator's base you check your reflection in the convex security mirror, mounted on a walkway bend. You're wearing a cap and carrying a lone worker alarm partially obscured by an orange tabard. You glance up at the fluorescent tubing, which is locked in a continual state of flicker. In your line of sight there's an Anti-Fascist sticker which reads CLOSE DOWN THE BNP. It's been overlaid with swastikas and the words NEED MORE NAZIS. This, in turn, has been overlaid with the words *PAKI POWER*.

You notice Sandra out of the corner of one eye. She's wheeling her pram along the platform.

'Hi Sandra, how's it *going?*'

She seems different. A little disturbed. You ask her if everything's okay.

'Everything's *fine*', she says, walking away.

You make out another familiar figure in the distance. You've turfed her out before, several times

End of the Line

before, but she keeps returning like a recurrent infection. She's dressed in a babushka scarf festooned with jumping rose-petals.

Lying recumbent across her lap with a dummy plugged into its mouth is a sleeping toddler beside a boy who looks like he's just stepped out of a Far Side cartoon. The beggar pushes a cardboard sign towards you:

'AM FROM REFUGGEE. HAVE 2 BEBYZ, 4 CHILDERZ, 6 BRADERS, NO MUNEEY. NO NAPPYZ TO BABYEE. TANKU.' Your radio rattles.

'Charlie-Tango 9. Turf that one *out*, yeah? I can see her on camera 5.'

'Charlie-Tango-9, *received*, over…'

You have a disturbing thought. Could it be that this sleeping toddler before you has been pumped full of drink, or even drugs? Are toddlers internationally trafficked, perhaps? You dismiss the idea as ludicrous and eject the beggars. As the toddler is carried away, it doesn't wake up or stir.

Walking on, you notice a customer information board and wonder when the term *'passenger'* fell out of favour.

You recall being sent on a three-day course about political correctness two years ago. LUL had received complaints at the time, including a specific one from an old Jewish lady in Golders Green who complained that *DUE* TO sounded too much like

End of the Line

JEW TO. From that point on, management encouraged the use of synonyms such as OWING TO or BECAUSE OF. WHITE BOARD was also deemed racist and was substituted for CUSTOMER INFORMATION BOARD. The word ALIGHT was also replaced because it sounded too much like something was on fire.

You glance up at the dot-matrix destination describer. It says: '*Message waiting….*' Below it is a sticker with the image of a black sheep and the caption 'DISOBEY'. The rails emit a wince as a train curves into the platform and draws to a standstill in a pneumatic hiss of air brakes. Its doors trundle open as passengers individuate themselves from each other. A mother turns to a wandering child dressed in a romper suit. 'Come here, you!'

Standing on the diamond marker as the train idles in the platform, you flick a two-note chime.'*BING-BONG!* … and then make a long line PA against a backdrop of acoustic feedback.

'Is this thing gan *north?*'

'Yep.

'You're a wee *gem!*'

You press the 'PUSH-TO-TALK' button.

'MURDER-*DO*', you say into the Tannoy as soon as the signal nods. It's close enough to 'mind the doors' and nobody seems to notice.

The train pulls away with an ascending click and

End of the Line

soon disappears through the horseshoe arch of the tunnel, accompanied by sizzles of electrical arcing. You remove the P.A. key and wave at the bill-poster guy who's scraping down old *'bills'* and sponging down new ones with a long-handled brush.

'Which way for *Bogna*, son?'

You apply the S.E.P. procedure (Somebody Else's Problem) and direct him towards two co-workers who are casually shooting the breeze by the tunnel headwall as someone, an 'undesirable', hands out 'TASTY LAUNCH PARTY' flyers advertising 'a night of full-on trance *madness*'.

'Dropping things is a sign you're in *love*' says a woman, dropping something.

It's time for gate-line duty now, so you head up and step off the cowl of the upper escalator as a little girl says to her friend: 'Last one through the gates is *fat!*'

You're entering the strike zone now. It's about to start, all the customer questions, the laddish posturing, the inverted snobbery, the foul-mouthed comments, the gate-line ogling, the homecoming hordes. You inhale and stride forward.

'Where's the way *out*?' someone asks, setting down their 'NISA SATISFACTION' bag.

'Where's *Bromley* street?' says someone else, setting down their 'SAINSBURY'S, WHERE *GOOD* FOOD COSTS *LESS*' bag.

End of the Line

'Come round *this* way, darlin'!', Big Pete says, 'busy t'day with the *football*, innit?'

The arm paddles of the pneumatic gates are thumping and crashing as a man carrying a bag with 'FRESH FRUIT DAILY' written across it, approaches you. 'Oy *mate!*' he says, 'me *ticket* don't work…I think I've got a dodgy strip or *summink*..'

'*Excuse* me pal', someone else cuts in. 'I've lost me *ticket*….oh *shit!*...And now I've broken me *glasses!*'

'OY! *Transport* geeza! The ELECTROLYSIS on me *ticket* don't work!'

'*Electrolysis* means *hair* removal', you helpfully point out.

'Well, it's basically *fucked*, mate.'

'*Corrupted*, maybe?'

'No, *fucked*, mate.'

'Oy *mate!* Someone's just stole the wheels off of me *bicycle*… do us a favour and let us *froo!*'

You let the whole world and his dog through the courtesy gate and turn to face your colleagues. 'All right my son?' one of them says.

'*Sayin'* Holmes?', another says.

'Hello CHAPS', you say. 'You alright?'

'*CHAPS?* Ain't that summink you get on your *lips?*'

There's a collective giggle.

End of the Line

'What *choo* been up ta, *posh* face? Slappin' the bum cheeks with the ol' *ball* baggage, was ya?'

'I went and saw some *artwork* last night, actually. Some *paintings*.'

'Oh, *artwork*', one of them says, mimicking your middle class accent.

'Oh, yeah? *Blindin"*, says another. 'Didja get to keep the *negatives?*'

Your attention drifts to a colleague cocooned in his glass-fronted sentry box, a box that looks like a standing coffin. The person inside is reading The Sun, which is half hidden between the pages of the weekly Traffic Circular.

Meanwhile, Pete is busy leaning against one of the gate paddles and leafing through a booklet entitled **'WE'RE GREAT ON THE GATES'**, the subheading of which reads: 'Are you a gate-line greeter or a gate-line grumbler?' as a woman wearing a 'LION CUB SANCTUARY' T-shirt approaches him and asks to be let through the courtesy gate.

'All right then, *lovely!*'

'Don't call me *'lovely'*, you *twat!*', she says, giving him a withering look.

'No need t'be givin' it all that *mouth*, darlin'! I ain't *dun* nuffink!'

A female passenger with a 'BHS – IT'S HAPPENING' bag slung over her shoulder, walks

End of the Line

up, pauses.

'I know what you guys *do*', she says, addressing Big Pete. 'You look at all the girls who come through and think, 'I wonder what *that* one's like in *bed?..Don't* you, I bet, *ay?*'

'Look at dat POOM-POOM, *boy!*' a colleague called Rudy says, 'KISS-ME *RUSS* CLUT!'

'Nice *Wutherings*, look', Pete says. 'Nice *Afro* puff there!'

'*Wutherings?*' you ask.

'Wuthering heights…*tights*… it's right up 'er *crack*. Boy!' he says, now into his radio.

'I'd give 'er a solid ol' *portion*, over!' SNAP!

'Sink the ball into the *19th!*' SNAP!

'SUPERVISOR TA *GATELINE*, OW JA MOTHERS *GROW* YA? HOW MANY BLEEDIN' *TIMES?!*'

'Sorry, gov!...Ooh my *days!* Mornin' *darlin*'', says Pete.

The woman he's addressing wrinkles her nose, walks past him with a sneer.

'Fucking *SCRUBBER!*', Pete says, following her with his eyes.

Another woman passes through the gates, causing Pete's head to turn.

End of the Line

'TREACLE! *CHICKETTA!* BONITTA…*'ello!*… SUZY? BRENDA? SHELLY? TINA? *TRISH?*…'

This is Pete's technique. Doing a roll call of random names until he stumbles on the right one.

You press the *'broadcast'* button on your radio and request a P.N.R *(physical needs relief)*. The supervisor gives you the heads up with a '*10-4, over!*'

It's rush hour now and the commuter troops have descended, all heading back to their various ant hills in the suburbs. With the arrival of peak traffic, the crowds begin to converge like a hungry tumour devouring its way through the station. You let a lady through the courtesy gate with a recalcitrant child who's tethered to an anti-wander harness. As you reclose the gate, you hear a metallic ring as an elderly gentleman raises a wooden cane. The shaft of his cane is decorated with shield mounts and has a thumb-activated bicycle bell on its handle. 'Let us through, son.' You nod and let him through using your universal gate pass. '*Thank* you, inspector', he says, tapping the cane's ferrule on the floor.

'*Attention!* This is a *CONTRACTOR* CALL…'

Buntiya, who's kicking back against the gate-line beside you, jumps to attention.

'Izzat di *red*-yo? Izzat a call fo *me?*'

'Yeah.'

'Okee. *Tanks*'

'Buntiya..', Pete says, leaning into him.

End of the Line

'*Uh?*'

'You're fifty-*nine* and you're *still* cleaning *khazis*, sort it *out* mate!'

Pete hands Buntiya his radio handset.

'Bess. Dis is Buntiya, *ova!*'

'Buntiya, the platforms are *LITERARY*. Newspapers all *over* the flamin' gaff. Can you *sort* it, yeah?' SNAP!

'*Okee* boss…' SNAP!

'And one *more* fing, Buntiya…' SNAP!

'*Eh?*' SNAP!

'There's a *code V* liquid *spillage* near the eastbound *tail*-wall.' SNAP!

'Okee, bess. Is dis spillage *clean?*, like *water?* or *dirty*, like *vomit?*'

'It's a *protein* spill, Buntiya, get me *drift?*'

'*What*, bess?'

'It's a pavement *pizza*, yeah?…'

'*Pizza?*'

'It would've been *once*, yeah…'

'Is *Smelly?*'

'It's *Vomit*, Buntya. It don't smell of no French *perfume*. It's a *slip* hazard, so, get a *move* on, *yeah?*' SNAP!

End of the Line

'*Okee*, but I muss tek di *lunch* brek first, das de *ting*. I juss take di lunch and den I go down to di *pla*-fon.'

'Buntya, *BUNTY*, I NEEDJA to *desist* from eatin' your salt fish and plantain stew-ups for now, *yeah*? It's *urgent*, you *get* me? Besides, it's the *peak* now, an' *all*. We got punters all *over* the gaff.' SNAP!

Buntiya shakes his head, marshals his mop and plastic LUCY bucket and scurries to the platforms. The supervisor comes back on the radio.

'Delta *fourteen!*...Don't chew wind me up an' *all* son!... REMOVE that *HAT* from your *ARMPIT* and put it on your *HEAD*, where it *BELONGS!*...I'm watchin' ya through the *winda*.' SNAP!

You look at your watch, it's clocking off time. The supervisor hasn't called your name, so you head to his office. On his desk lies a RHINO'S REVENGE calendar and a copy of *The Station Circular*. You can see him from behind, fingering the tracking ball on the on-panel camera which is trained like an artillery piece on a woman and her dreadlocked Hungarian sheepdog. The supervisor hits zoom, sharpens the image, expands it until it fills his monitoring screen and watches the woman minus her sheepdog as she files past a sign which reads:

'CAUTION: YOU ARE BEING *WATCHED*. As part of our commitment to your safety, we have video-linked cameras for monitoring purposes only. This may include off-site image and audio'. The cameras flip into sequence mode, tracking the woman as she ascends from platform to ticket hall, and then out of camera shot.

'Er...gov, Is this a bad *time?*', you ask.

'*Ay?*', he asks, startled.

'You forgot to *call* me, guv, my shift's *over*, I want to sign *out*.'

'Hang *about*, Peregrine, I'm *busy*', he says, hitting a button market DELETE SCREEN.

'Er...Echo-*8*,...come *in* echo-8!' he says into his angled microphone. Echo-8 is Sid's call sign.

'Receivin' loud and clear, go *ahead*...'

'*Alright* down there on platform *3?* No *trouble* or nuffink? I heard there were '*old ups* down at *Oxo* on the *Vic*.'

'Yeah, guv, everyfink's fine, *except*...'

'Except *what?*'

'Except there's some geezer *filming* down 'ere. Is he allowed to *do* that?' SNAP!

'No he *ain't*, Sid!' SNAP!

'I've just told the geeza that if he ain't filming for *commercial* purposes, then it's *okay*, like'

'How can you *believe* him, Sid?'

'How ja *mean* guv?' SNAP!

'COME *ON*, Einstein. *Question:* How d'you *KNOW* this geezer ain't filming for commercial purposes?

End of the Line

You can't take 'im on his *say-so*. If a geezer had a *bomb* in his pockit, he wouldn't say: 'Hey, mate, I got a *bomb* in me pockit', *would* he? Get where I'm *goin'* with this, Sid? If this geeza ain't got written *permission*, he can't *film*, full *stop*. SIMPLES. Besides, the travelling public have a *right* to *privacy*.' SNAP!

'*Righto*, guv.' SNAP!

'By the way echo-8, 'ave you managed to sort that DOOR thing out yet?'

'The *door* thing?…That's a *negative*, guv.' SNAP!

'What d'ya *mean* 'that's a *negative*'?' *SNAP!*

'Well, I mean, not *exactly*, if ya know what I *mean*.' SNAP!

'*No*, Sidney, I have *no* idea what you mean. You're being as clear as *mud* 'ere' SNAP!

'I'm not sure how to attach the *whatsit* to the *thingamajig*' SNAP!

'*No* Sidney, *NO!* I didn't say *attach* it! I said *remove* it! Are you mutton, or what?'

'Guv, I don't know how to *remove* it, over.' SNAP!

'Use your *initiative!* D'ya know what '*initiative*' means? Got a *dictionary?* And while yer *at* it, can you put number *2* on the *up*. I did *ask* someone to do it, but they OBVIOUSLY *forgot!* SNAP!

'Bravo-9 to *base!* SNAP!

End of the Line

'*Standby* bravo-9!' SNAP!

'So, echo-8, Sid, is that an *affirmative,* or *what?*' SNAP!

'*Fink* so, gov!' SNAP!

'Well, I'll phone down in a few minutes to make sure you know what you're *doin'*. The phone'll be that *plastic object* ringing *behind* ya. And one *more* fing, Sid. Did ya put that VIP on the *train?*' SNAP!

'The *VIP?*' SNAP!

'Yeah, the VIP…Did you *assist* him, okay, over?' SNAP!

'The VIP with the sunglasses? *That* bloke? That **VERY IMPORTANT** *PERSON* bloke?' SNAP!

'*No*, Sidney, *No!* VIP stands for '*VISUALLY IMPAIRED PERSON*'. Don't tell me ya didn't *know* that!' SNAP!

'Guv,…er, I made sure the geezer got on the *northbound*, over.' SNAP!

'The *northbound??* He was going *south*, you MUPPET!' SNAP!

'I fought you said he wanted to go *north*, over.' SNAP!

'Your *HEART's* in the right place, Sidney, but your *BRAIN* obviously ain't. You don't put a *blind* gentleman on a train without *asking* where he's *goin'*, just like you don't put *leather* and *wool* in a *washing* machine, do you see what I'm *getting'* at?' SNAP!

End of the Line

'I didn't *know* he were blind, guv. You said he were a *VIP*.'

'He *were* a bleedin' VIP, ya *ploker!*'

'Bravo-9 to base, you *receivin'?*'

'*Standby,* Bravo-9!'

The supervisor reaches for the phone.

'Hello, *CAMDEN?* Listen. One of me NOB'EADS has stuck a *blind* gentleman on the wrong *train*. I know, I *know*. You can't get the *staff* no more, *can* ya? Listen, Fred, if a VIP turns up wandering about with a white *stick*, could you do us a *favour* and put him on the right *train?* He wants to go *south*, not *north*. Via the *Cross*, yeah. *Tad-ar*, Fred.'

'Hang *about*, Peregrine', he says to you. 'Go *ahead*, Bravo-9!'

'Bravo-9 t'base, come *in* base!' SNAP!

'I *said* I was receivin' you, over! I ain't *mutton*, what *is* it, Bravo-nine?' SNAP!

'I've completed me section *12* checks, guv.'

'Well *done*, Bravo-9. Come up and I'll give you a *gold star* and a *paper hat*.' SNAP!

'No, I *meant*, do I deserve a *fag* break now, over?' SNAP!

'As long as it's only five minutes this time, not fifteen, yeah?'

End of the Line

'By the *way*, Roge, any delays on the *Pic?* A customer's asking, and I ain't got no *clue*, and I can't get through to the 'ol *man…*'

'Well, according to Echo-8 we ain't *got* none, but I haven't *heard* nothin', so I wouldn't bet me *life* on it, like.'

'Oscar-12 to base, *hello?*'

'Oscar-*12?*.. We ain't *got* no Oscar-12! Who the flamin' heck's *THIS?*...What's your *call* sign and *location* caller?!*Identify* yourself!'

'Wos the *score* someone? *Anyone?*', Pete says into his radio. What follows is a fusillade of radio exchanges.

'It's FREE *NIL* TO MAN-*U!*'

'That's a big *ten-four* little bunny!'

'Big bear to *little* bear, what was that score again, *over?*'

'Bunny to *speedbird*, it's THREE-NIL! Do you *copy?*'

'Speedbird to Bunny. *Repeat!*'

'Tango-Charlie-*Niner*. Mike Uniform November is a three-nil *Whiskey.*'

'BASE TO ALL STAFF! *ENOUGH!* What *is* this? *Desist*, yeah? Keep them airwaves *clear!*'

Lyndon shakes his head, looks at you. 'What *you* waitin' for, Peregrine? Ain't you got no *'OME* to go to?'

End of the Line

'I was waiting for you to *call* me, so I could sign *out*. You were *late* callin' me.'

'*Late?* That's a bit flamin' *rich*, coming from *you*. Go on, sign your radio back *in* and get the 'ell *out* of here.'

On the way up to street level, you're accosted by a guy with eyes like potholes selling The Big Issue. '*Psst!* Come *'ere!* Let you into a little *secret*, mate. Heroin's better than *sex*…only thing *is,* I have to *smoke* it now 'cos I've knackered me *veins*', he says, rolling back one sleeve, then the other. 'Here, *look*, compare *mine* to *yours*', he says, in a display of bravado.

True enough. You notice he has no radial arteries, no *veins*.

'Well, *see*, I was injecting 3 to 4 times a *day*, until me veins began to *disappear,* mate.'

'*Right.*'

'-And the cold turkey was like…*imagine*, mate, catching yellow *fever*, *malaria* and *typhoid* all at the same *time*, all rolled into *one.*'

You shrug, nod sympathetically, exit slowly, head home.

End of the Line

CHAPTER FOUR

You're at home, slumped in front of the TV and trying not to think about the hamster wheel of tedium that is the reality of working inside a tube station. You're looking for mind-numbing distractions from a mind-numbing job by flipping TV channels until you find something vaguely interesting, which you do. You find a programme about an artist's attempts to recreate Stonehenge using refrigerators. Hotpoints, Smegs, Electroluxes, they're all arranged into one giant, Druidic circle. The installation's titled FRIDGEHENGE.
You flip channels after the programme finishes, locate a bit of trashy entertainment. It's love confessions on TRISHA and a guy called Lee hasn't been there for Sharon. He prefers to go out on wild benders with his mates to being stuck at home with Sharon and their baby, Topsy.

After the episode finishes, you watch another, titled *'My gang's my blood'* in which a teenage hoodlum is being asked why he's joined a gang. The teen has drawn features and a baseball cap on the wrong way round.

'So…why don't you attend *school?*'

'No *point*…'

'No *point?* Why?'

Trisha's face is mapped with concern, the studio audience is murmuring. There's a widespread hush,

End of the Line

a pregnant pause as everyone awaits the teenager's response.

'*DUNNO.*'

Trisha nods her head empathically, asks what he does on the streets.

'I don't do *NUTTIN*' on the streets', he says, his body language defensive.

There's a sudden drum roll as a curtain slides back. The audience is clapping and hooting as four surprise guests step forward. It's a group of rap artists called 'The Execution Squad'.

Tears well up in the teen's eyes. They're clearly his heroes. Trisha pokes her roving mic into the teen's face.

'So, what do you *think?*'

'Youz *JOKIN*' me, innit? De *Execution* Squad? Oh, my *days!* I ain't seen dem boys in *time*, blood… and now I see dem lot in *real* life? Oh, my *days!*'

After getting some vox pop reactions from random members of the studio audience, Trisha hands the mic over to a member of the squad, who approaches the teen with a shuffling gait.

'*Listen*, bruv… de *BLING*, de turf wars, de hangin' wid de *posse*, de *mash* ups, dem boys will *SLEW* ya, I swear *dumb*. Leave dat life, ain't much *good* getting' bare blazed on *skins*, yeah? And doze boys are *long*, bruv, *long!* Leave your *ends*, get me? But don't *VEX* boy, else you'll end up getting' *shanked*, innit?'

End of the Line

The audience hoots as the words 'CALL TRISHA'S DILEMMA LINE!' Flashes across the screen.

Immac, another member of the squad, steps forward. He's got the whole rap shuffle down pat. With a thick gold chain slung round his neck, gold caps on the front of his teeth and the tongues of his sneakers curled forward, he sidles up to the teen.

'DON'T hang wid dem *fuckboys*, NUMB *sayin'?* Avoid DOZE *blades* an' dem homie *bluds*. ISS all JUS fuckboy *hard* shit, na *UM* sayin'? *Safe*, yeah?'

Pioneer, another member, steps forward now. His swagger borders on the theatrical.

'*Yo!*', he says, exchanging a fist tap with the kid. He's a Yank. He pushes a pair of mirrored aviators up, places them high on his forehead, shuffles forward.

'Let's *kick* the habit, homeboy, let's *kick* it, yo! Yo mama wants to be *proud* of chew and I'm a bust yo *chops*, homie, if yo don't quit yo high-rollin'-dumb-arse-*horseshit!*'

The programme makers have bleeped out the numerous swearwords, but you manage to lipread the word mutherfucker on Pioneer's lips.

You flip channels. It's an episode of Eden's Daytime Chat Show and there's an obese woman on the show who's having problems with her 14-year old daughter. The mother is sitting on stage, in front of a big screen which reads 'MOMS WHO HATE THEIR CHILDREN'. She's sitting opposite the avuncular host Dr. Eden Hay.

End of the Line

'*Heck...*', she begins, 'she *trash* talks me an' she bars *money* and don't give none of it *back.*'

'Why don't you just *talk* to her, sensibly, *quietly*, Tammy?

'*Why?*'Cos them tantrums come the hell out of her like a *power* dump, Dr Eden.'

Dr. Eden takes a moment, steeples his fingers, takes on an expression of concern.

'This girl needs your *love*, Tammy. Listen to her *heart*, Tammy, listen to her *soul*…'

'To *heck* with her heart and *soul!* She's fulla *excuses*, Dr. Eden! An' every damn person from Franklin County to Fort Greely's got their *darn* fine *excuses!*'

The camera pans dramatically to a woman in the studio audience who's misty-eyed before cutting back to the stage where tears are glistening on Tammy's cheeks as Dr. Eden hands her a handkerchief embossed with the logo *DAYTIME WITH DOC EDEN*.

'This girl does more damage t'me than a *twister* ever could, Dr. Eden…I mean, where's she *at?*…'

'It's *okay*, Tammy, it's *okay*', Dr. Eden says, resting a hand on Tammy's trembling wrist.

'I *juss* want ma daughter t'quit *acting up*, is *all*….'

'*Tammy*', Dr. Eden says with an unwavering look, cupping her hands in his own. 'I want you to *listen*… and to listen real *good* now...'

```
End of the Line
```

You flip channels again. It's baseball and a close game for the Boston Red Sox. *'The fellers are acquitting themselves well'*, the announcer is saying as the camera cuts to the studio anchor who, with the aid of a jabbing finger, tells viewers to stay tuned because it's coming right up after a quick commercial break.

You flip channels again, to a programme about toilet innovations from Tokyo, featuring the famous *'Sound princess'* said to aid slow transit colons with its canny use of dulcet Autumn birdsong. And then you fall asleep.

End of the Line

CHAPTER FIVE

The next morning you're on the platforms. Gracing the front of a poster is the image of an albino lab rat, overlaid with the caption:

IT'S NOT ONLY CANCER SURGEONS WHO HAVE WHITE COATS AND SAVE LIVES. Across the poster, someone's scrawled:

'All *vivisectors* should undergo a session of *electrical torture* while under the influence of muscle relaxants and pain enhancing drugs. This rat is a pain-perceiving organism with a C.N.S like yours. DO YOUR CHILDREN *REALIZE* KIND-LOOKING DOCTORS IN WHITE COATS KILL SMALL *ANIMALS???*'You walk on, past a poster about safety on the tube. The words SAFETY FIRST are captioned in bold, but someone's crossed out the word 'SAFETY' and written *'MONEY'*.

You see a figure in the distance scuttling along the platform and follow discretely as the emaciated, shaven-headed shape sprays a nearby wall with an aerosol can. As the figure turns to face you, there's a hint of recognition. You know this face. You've seen it somewhere before.

Sandra? Could it be *Sandra?* You last saw Sandra a month ago, maybe more. Her face is *ghost-like* now.

'*Sandra?*'

No response. The figure scuttles off, mouse-like. You approach the freshly-sprayed wall. It reads:

End of the Line

'SANDRA IS A PROUD *BOTTOM*, LOOKING FOR GOOD *TOPPERS*, CONTACT SANDRA. PAIN=PLEASURE, GIRL *2*.'

On the floor in front of you is a pile of litter, comprised of the following: The skeletal remains of a City Fried *Buffalo* wing, an empty bag of *'PREMIUM BANANAS'*, a half-eaten *Casey Jones Special,* some sort of fiery religious tract, a carton of 'extra value- *absolutely no sugar added'* Ribena, a box of Sovereign cigarettes, fruit creams in a variety of fun flavours, an *I'm lovin' It* Egg Mcflurry and a scrunched-up letter which you pick up. It reads:

'Hi Fran. How was lunch? So, you and Michael are still *fighting*? Maybe a bit of sexual *tension??*(Joke). What did he say when you asked him to Seaton's farewell? Didn't he say something about you guys *arguing?* Have u heard from Adam/ busboy *again?* You should just *forget* about busboy! He must be *desperate* trying to date a drunk girl he met on the number 25 night bus, *no?*

I said we should give guys a *chance,* but I've decided that I'm not going to *kiss* guys anymore when I'm *drunk*. I always regret it the next day, cos it's usually a guy I'd never want to *see* again. Hey, you should find out if *Tom* has a girl, you're both Harry Potter freaks. *(Ha-Ha!)* Well, *see* ya!Shelly.'You discard the letter and, stepping back, accidentally knock into a bum standing behind you.

'Don't you *push* me!'

'*Sorry*, mate!'

End of the Line

'I'm not going to be *pushed* or *controlled* by people or bills or *injections*.'

'Sorry *again*, mate.'

You notice he's clutching a note in his hand. It reads:I'm not religious, but can you ask some church if they can give me *money?* Can you give me 5-6 pounds for food? I, myself, stand for the truth. You *understand?* Is that *clear?* Because I have all the *answers!* Born with *power*. Year 1955.'

A little later, as you book off and leave work, you run into a woman hovering by the station exit who promptly pushes a sprig of heather into your nostrils.

'It's for the *children*, bless their *hearts*…'

'*What* children?'

'The poor *little* 'uns'

'Who *are* these children?'

'One *pound!* Come *on!* Giv us a pound for the children, poor *things!*'

'One *pound?* For a sprig of *heather?*'

'Heather, my lovely, will bring you luck in love, my sweet!'

'I'm *okay*', you say, sidestepping her, but she blocks your path. 'It's *lucky* heather, white, *rare*, come *on*, me lovely!'

She's holding a bunch of sprigs, each tightly bound

       End of the Line

in Bacofoil.

'It's *bad* luck not t'take heather from a gypsy *traveller*, me darlin', don't you *know* that?'

You admire the woman's entrepreneurial spirit.

'No, I *didn't*.'

'This lucky heather's white as the *moon*, white as the stars in *heaven*.'

'Are you a *charity?*'

'*Yes*, love. Charity for the *little* ones, look, this is Highland heather, my lovely. *Smell* it…go on! Take a *whiff*, it's for the *children*….'

Sidestepping her, you think about all the disparate annoyances you're forced to navigate on the streets of London: chuggers with clipboards, beggars blockading cash machines, Jehovah's Witnesses straddling tube entrances, and *more.*

End of the Line

CHAPTER SIX

Before the commencement of your shift the following day, you pop into a supermarket to grab a lunchtime meal deal. It's not a simple operation. Before you find the relevant aisle, you're forced to negotiate your way past a pop-star poster rack featuring Cliff Richard, his silk shirt unbuttoned, a fluffy dog at his feet. Then past a topless Robbie Williams, his hand suggestively caressing the rim of a cowboy hat.

As you arrive at the station, meal deal in hand, you notice a board with the following message: 'THERE ARE NO REPORTED SERVICE PROBLEMS THIS MORNING'. The word *'yet'* has been added in biro.

Soon you're back on the platforms.

'Excuse me sir, for ze *cough* und *garden?*'

'*That* way, madam.'

'Is ze *blue* collar line, *ja?*'

You nod. The tourist departs. Your radio splutters, but it's just static interference and random noise, probably one of your colleagues messing with the depress button.

You walk past a busker with unkempt hair and wispy sideburns. He's singing *'Streets of London'* in synch with a dancing, swaying puppet.

'Base t'Charlie-Tango-9, come *in!* 'SNAP!

End of the Line

'Receiving', you say.

'Time for your *grub* break, yeah?'

As you enter the messroom with your shop-bought sandwich, you notice some new posters and pictures tacked to the staffroom noticeboard. There are the usual *RMT* union notices and several photos of deep tube and sub-service rolling stock with their discrete liveries hanging beside a notice which reads:

'NORTHERN & PIC LINE CARNIVAL FUN DAY. VENUE: TOOTING BEC SPORTSGROUND. INFLATABLE BOXING, BOUNCY CASTLES, DISCO, BUCKING BRONCOS, SEGA ROADSHOW BUS. ADULTS AND KIDS ALL WELCOME.'

Beside the poster is a handwritten notice with the heading: 'Fun maths teasers'. It reads:

Question 1: Dave's Cortina does 20 miles to the gallon. If Dave travels at a constant speed of 5 miles per hour for 40 minutes, how much petrol will he use before he receives a police caution? *Question 2, part 1* (this is a *2-part* question):

Del lives in Bermondsey and has to travel 100 miles each day to get to work. If he travels 60 miles per hour, how much time does he waste each week?

Question 2, part 2: And how much *extra* time would he waste if he detoured 20 miles to pick up *Eileen?*
Question 3:

Chas purchases a football club for 32 million. He

invests a further 33 million per year for 10 years. Assuming his 'mate' Arthur syphons off 320,000 a week for 3 years, and during all this time the trophy-cabinet remains empty, how bankrupt is the club going to be within 5 years?'

ANSWERS ON A POSTCARD.

End of the Line

CHAPTER SEVEN

You're on platform patrol and notice an advert for the new McDonald's hotdog. To the left of the golden arches, someone's scribbled 'VO', and to the right, 'IT'. Your radio vibrates.

'Base ta Charlie-Tango-9, come *in!*'

'Receiving…'

'We needja ta cover a shift in the *booking* office. Someone's gone Tom and *Dick*, ova.'

'You need me *now?*'

'That's an *affirmative*. You're a *multifunc*, yeah? Come up *pronto*, over and out!' SNAP!

'On my *way*, guv, over.'

You head to the booking hall area and past a line of passengers waiting stoically behind a serving window. You thump a door 3 times with the toe of your Doc Martens until an observation hatch, a kind of spy hole slides sideways to reveal a chink of light, followed by an eye. 'It's *me*', you gesture before the door swings open. You step inside, passing a mall-mounted decal emblazoned with the message: **'MAKE FRIENDS WITH A TICKET MACHINE'**. The interior of the ticket office is a mess of filing cabinets and metal card-frame drawers. Your colleague says 'Alright?' to which you respond in kind.

End of the Line

The radio is on, pumping out MOR standards. 'Can't beat a bit a Bon *Jovi*', he says as he hops back onto the swivel stool at the illuminated window, a series of discontinued teacakes on the countertop beside him. The ticket clerk is Eric, a cantankerous and gaunt-looking individual with a heavy brow, a lantern jaw and hair that looks as though it's been dyed with boot polish. He looks like Frankenstein's monster, minus the bolts. Eric has a problem with the public. It's a detailed loathing rooted in the unceasing need on the part of the passengers to ask stupid questions, particularly *'them foreign fuckers'*.

The last time your services were required in the booking office was on an inauspicious Monday, after you'd popped a tab of LSD at the weekend. The effects hadn't subsided during that morning stint on the window, but you have a hazy recollection that someone had asked for a travel-card and that you'd printed the ticket, stared at it, perused its texture, turned it over in your hand. Something didn't seem right, so you printed another, but that didn't seem right either. You printed a third. Same problem. Soon, you were overcome by an all-enveloping, frenzied bout of panic. The sweat kept coming, dripping onto the arbitrary pile of cards in front of you. You couldn't fathom the numbering system. Was one a date and one a price? If so, which was which? With an ominous-looking queue stretched out in front of you, doubling, tripling, the panic kept rising in ever-increasing waves.

On another morning, after a weekend of marijuana indulgence, you were called into one of the station's rooms to provide a urine sample as part of the company's policy of springing unannounced drug and alcohol tests on their frontline employees. You recall the nurse saying 'Help yourself

End of the Line

to water if you can't oblige.' The nurse collected your specimen in a sample bottle before signing the necessary chain of custody forms. You had to provide two samples. One was to be kept in safe storage, the other to be send for independent analysis. You have no idea whether by accident or divine intervention, but you passed the test.

The memories fade as you let your gaze drift across the booking office. Sellotaped to the inside of the excess fares window is a sign which reads 'DO YOU BANG ON THE WINDOWS OF BANKS AND POST OFFICES? *NO?* THEN WHY DO IT *HERE?*'Beside the sign is a more visual one, comprising a mini hangman's noose hung with hazard tape as a cautionary warning to potential fare dodgers and ticketless travellers.

A woman sidles up to Eric's assistance window. She stares at him through the glass divide, a question forming on her lips.

'Are you *open?*', she asks.

'What does it *look* like, love?'

'Just a *question.* Do you think this one'll do for me *photo-card?*' she says, holding up an over-exposed headshot taken in the station's PHOTO ME booth.

'You shouldn't expect a David *Bailey* off of them things, darlin'…*next?* Next customer?!'

'*Single!*'

'*Are* you love? I'm not *surprised*. A single *what?*'

'A single *ticket.*'

End of the Line

'To *where*, darlin'?'

'To Wood Green.'

'That's *better*, love. I need *specifics*, not *non*-specifics. *Next?!*'

'Can I have some *change*, pal?'

'We don't *give* out change, mate. There are 5 *banks* out there. *Next?*'

'But I need *change!*'

'I said we don't *give* out change. Go down to the newsagent's on the corner. They'll tell ya to fuck off, and *all*. Next?'

'One *ticket*, please!'

'Destination?'

'The *tube*.'

Eric stares blankly through the guard glass. 'I require a *DESTINATION*.'

'I ain't going *no* place. Not *specifically*…'

'We're talkin' at cross *purposes* 'ere, mate. What do you *mean?*'

It's a visiting tourist, a Yank. He points to the circle line on a pocket map, flattening it against the window.

'What's this *yella* line called?'

'That's the *circle* line, mate.'

End of the Line

'Well, *okay.* I just wanna *ride* that *SUCKER* right *around*.'

'This ain't a *merry*-go-round, mate. You need an endpoint destination.'

'A *specific* one?'

'Yeah', Eric says, turning to you and mouthing '*wanker*'.

An American couple, both donning tall baseball caps, rock up at the window.

'Which way for the *green* train?'

'Platform *3* for the *district*.'

'*Thanks*, pal.'

You prepare a float by emptying one of the coin hoppers and filling your money drawer with notes and change, then shove a roll of uncut tickets into the handling slot on the till machine. After checking the level of paper-stock in the till's tally roll, you hop onto a blue stool, seat yourself behind anger-proof glass and switch on the mic and induction loop. As soon as your 'ASSISTANCE' sign is illuminated, you release the roller blind and just as immediately, passengers begin to descend on you in a surge of renewals, replacements, requests and questions. And like the trained seal that you are, you deal with them one at a time until there's a lull. For a few moments, you're just sitting at the window, eating a roll and reading Bukowski's Post Office until someone appears.

End of the Line

'Are you *open?*'

'I *am*. And you, are you *Australian?*' you ask the woman in front of you, who you suspect is Australian.

'No... I just got *hay* fever...I'm *English*', the woman says, unblocking a nostril and pushing a £20 note through the window tray, a note which is dye-stained and mutilated. Across it, someone's scribbled: 'BUY THE BOYS A PIZZA, IT'LL SAVE U HAVING TO COOK!' You slide the £20 note into a note band and survey the snaking line of passengers that's suddenly appeared.

'Can you hurry *up*, mate? I'm late for *work!*', the man behind the woman says.

'How about a *coffee* sometime?' you teasingly suggest, as the woman looks into your face for a beat.

'Is this a *DATING* service or a *TICKET* booth?'

A New Zealander steps forward now. 'Kin I heave a one and TOE *TRECK* CARD?'

'I *knew* you were an antipode', you say, pulling the gooseneck mic towards you. 'I had a *gut* feeling.'

'Why's *THEET?*'

'Your *accent.*'

'I don't *HEAVE* in ICK-sent…by the way, sir, do you have a *PIN* I could borrow?'

'What, a *drawing* pin?'

'No. A *biro* PIN.'

'So, you *ARE* from New Zealand!'

'Not *exactly*. I was born in Poland, live in Sydney, grew up in New Zealand, then lived in New York by way of London, but I'll be in New Zealand again *soon*.'

'I see. Here for *work?*'

'No, I'm here to see my sister-in-law's sister. And to *study*.'

'What are you *studying?*'

'Fine Art.'

'That's what *I* studied, you'll end up in a booking office like *this* one, if you're not *careful*.'

'That would be truly *AWFUL!*'

'Are you a *model?*'

'Why, do I look *stressed?*'

'No, you look *airbrushed*.'

'You ought to get *out* more, but thanks.'

'Take care! Okay, next? Who's *next?* Yes, madam…'

A woman with long, curly, fake nails approaches your ticket booth. She buys a ticket with a fifty pound note and then struggles to retrieve the change, swiping at the dish with flailing nails.

'What's that, a *tip* and *overlay?*'

End of the Line

'*Nah!* Acrylic *extensions.* They got snap dragon *gel* over the top. *Like* 'em?'

You nod that you do very much like them as the next customer asks for a ticket to Cockfosters. You print the ticket and the passenger scoops it out of the tray.

'How do I *get* there?'

'*Where?*' you ask, your mind still anchored to the image of nails grappling with recalcitrant coins.

'You sold me a ticket to Cockfosters, *didn't* you?'

'Cockfosters is on platform *2*, but you need to *change*.'

You hop off the stool and walk the length and breadth of the office in time to serve the next passenger, who sounds Greek and explains that she wants to visit some interesting *plates* today.

You pull down your blind and take a longer breather while Eric takes over. You boil a kettle in the back and watch Eric at the front.

'*Good* morning', a passenger says.

'What's so *good* about it?'

The passenger shrugs, 'Can I have ONE please?'

'One *WHAT?* Me TELEPATHY skills are a bit *weak* this mornin'.'

'I want a *single*.'

```
End of the Line
```

'You're not *helpin'* yourself here, darlin'. A single *what?* I need *particulars.*'

'A single *ticket.*'

'I need a *destination*, love, I need *specifics*. You don't just walk into *Starbuck's* and ask 'em for a cup of *coffee*, although *you* probably do. We got all *sorts* of ticket types and medleys 'ere', love.'

'*Hampstead*', she says, handing Eric a scrunched up £10 note.

Eric prints out a ticket, counts up the change, makes a show of taking out a crisp, flat, pristine-looking £5 note from his money drawer, scrunches it into a tight little ball and drops the ball into the change dish in front of her.

There's a double rap on the excess fares window. Eric cranes his head.

'Old your *'ORSES* mate! If people *rush* me, I end up hittin' all the wrong *keys!*'

'I *can't* wait!' The man shouts back.

'Base to booking office assist, you got a *customer*, over!'

'Yeah, yeah, I can *see* that, I'm comin', *over!*'

Eric hops off his stool, strides up to the window.

'Where's the *FIRE* mate?'

'I'm waiting to be served, I'm in a *rush!*'

End of the Line

'As soon as somebody tells me to hurry *up*, I slow *down*.'

'You've served three people on the main window while I've been *standing* here…'

'Why was ya *knockin'?*'

'Because I've been waiting, I *told* you!'

'Well, this ain't a KNOCKING shop, you'll hafta wait your *turn*.'

'I've already *been* waiting 5 MINUTES!'

'You gotta buy your ticket *before* you travel, mate, not *after!* I don't like getting' off of me bum for someone who can't be *bovered* to buy a ticket before they *travel*.'

'5 minutes I've been here and *counting!*', the man says, flicking some change into the dish.

'*Listen*, mate, I *told* ya, you can't just *come* 'ere and buy a ticket from the *excess* winda, you'll hafta wait your *turn!*'

'How *long?*'

'As *long* as you would have to have waited at the other *end*, yeah?'

Eric throws you a look. 'These people are all *self, self, self!* They've got no common *courtesy!*'

'The ticket office was CLOSED when I started my *journey*, mate!'

Eric rolls his eyes, sells the guy a ticket. As he hands

End of the Line

him his change, he says: '*Fuck*youverymuch, sir!', before he slumps back down on the main window. A moment later, there's another knock at the window. Eric gets up again.

'Wos the *problem*, love?'

'I've lost my HUSBAND!'

'*What?*'

'We got *separated* when the train doors closed before I could get *on!*'

'What the bleedin' *'ell's* that got to do with *ME?*'

'PLEASE *HELP* ME, sir, I've lost my *husband!*'

'If I had a wife like *you*, darlin', I'd've lost you *too!*'

'PLEASE, can't you *help* me?'

'Go knock on the station supervisor's door over *there*, look. EEL 'elp ya darlin', *see?*'

'What does he *look* like?'

'He's a MIDGET with a peaked CAP and a gammy leg. Can't miss 'im for *toffee*, luv…'

Meanwhile, the queue is building on Eric's main window. A woman is waiting to be served, with a line snaking behind her.

'Any more *skunkin'* up from the drains behind ya, love? *Look* at it, look. They're like *flies*, them lot! *Millions* of them wantin' tickets.'

You wander into the anteroom to have another

End of the Line

breather. When you return, you notice that Eric's up to his usual thing. He has this money-making ruse that he uses on unsuspecting Japanese tourists. If they give him a pound, he covers it with his hand while distracting them with conversation. As they respond with nodding smiles, he holds up a ten pence coin. 'Sorry t'*say* this, but you give me *ten pence* not a *pound*, you owe me a *pound*.' There are always ensuing apologies, bowing and respectful nods. The Japanese tourists never suspect the mistake isn't of their own making, that someone would pull one over on them. Occasionally a Japanese tourist will freeze with momentary bewilderment and questioning eyes but then swiftly acquiesce in order to save face. It's a cultural convenience and a steady little earner for Eric.

You've witnessed other scams. Booking staff working in cahoots with barrier staff, working to resell paper tickets, always wary of 'traps', LUL employees posing as passengers, hoping to catch them red-handed. The way it works is this: A gate-line assistant lets a passenger through the gates, retains their ticket, hands the ticket to the clerk who then resells it or cancels it, then deducts the cash. You recall a colleague, always dishevelled-looking, always had his shirt open at the front who would use some of the proceeds of his till to repay outstanding loans. He had a younger girlfriend whom he'd lavish with gifts but the only way he could satisfy her materialistic expectations was by maintaining a deception. He'd pay large amounts of cash from his till into his bank and cover the missing cash with a cheque from a customer, the customer being himself. Once a fortnight he'd slope into the local bank beside the station in his dishevelled uniform, a

End of the Line

cloth bag hanging from his hand. He was able to keep ahead of himself for months until one day the bank became suspicious and arranged for a police officer to lie in wait. You never heard from him again.

You recall another colleague who insisted on helping you cash up at the end of your shift by counting what was in your money drawer. You naively assumed he was being helpful, but on more than one occasion you ended up with a debit on your account, and you weren't his only victim.

Eric's currently serving an uppity businessman.

'A right bleedin' stuffed shirt *this* one! They think they own the world but they don't own *nothing!*… And the bloke *behind?*…Sometimes I think I'm talkin' to me bleedin' *self!*'

'I'm confused about the *zones!*'

'Yeah? And *I'M* confused about why *YOU'RE* confused!'

'What's the difference between the *zones*…and what are the different *prices?* Do I need a one way or *return?*'

'Jesus, one *ticket*, 400 *questions!*'

The next passenger approaches. 'Could you spare one of them thingy holders?'

'A *ticket* wallet? You know mate, I'm fed *up* with people coming up an' asking: 'You have a *plastica?*', 'You have a *pocket?*' Drives me *crazy*, that does!'

The passenger smiles wanly as Eric turns on the

End of the Line

radio.

'Well, it's twenty-one minutes away from ten, playing your all-time favourite hits *back-to-back!*'

The American couple wearing the tall baseball caps from earlier on approach the window, huffing and puffing.

'Yes, mate?', Eric says.

'What in the hell is *wrong* with you people? *Huh?*'

'*Ay?* What are you *on* about?'

'We've been waitin' 45 minutes for a *train!*'

'What the *hell* d'ya mean?'

'You told us the green train was on platform *3!*'

'That's *right*, district line trains go from platform *3*. There are trains every 5 *minutes*. Don't lose your bleedin' rag with *me*, over nothing, mate!'

'We waited *45* minutes for a *green* train, mister! There were NO damn *green* trains, just *white* trains, no *green* trains! You been *messin'* with our heads and we want our damn *money* back!'

'Fuckin' *yanks!* Wos *wrong* with you people!'

You swiftly reopen your window as Eric, effing and blinding, redirects the American couple towards Lyndon's office and then slams his window blind shut.

A Jamaican guy in a beanie rocks forward, resting

End of the Line

one arm on the window ledge. 'Ey *mister!* I wanna travelcard *ting!*'

You tell the guy the price of the ticket.

'Expensive, *te rass*, DYAMN expensive!'

'That's the *price*, I'm afraid…'

'Forget it, me a *war-k!*'

You shrug your shoulders. The guy begins to walk away, but then changes his mind, turns back.

'Ey…mister…*ey!*', he says, 'Me-wan-aksk-you-gotta-ting-for-me-put-me *treen*-card-in?'

Someone else steps up to the window.

'Excuse me, could I have a ticket wallet *thingy?*'

You hand the guy his wallet thingy as he hands you a £10 note across which someone's scribbled: 'To Benjamin dear from Auntie Audrey'.

A woman with an Italian accent approaches. 'I couldn't take you out for a bowl of *spaghetti*, could I?' you joke.

'I got a boyfriend from *Sicily*, come *on!*', she jokes back.

An American, Redneck, wearing purple ear muffs approaches. She's accompanied by a younger woman. You presume they're mother and daughter. They request subway tokens.

'Ya wanna *know* somethin', buddy?'

```
End of the Line
```

'What's *that?*', you ask.

'When I first heard the name the *London Underground*, I thought it was a *terrorist* organisation.'

'An *easy* mistake to make.'

'I never knew it was a *transit* system 'til I came *t'England*. Anyway, which 'ROWT' t'git to LIE-CHESTER? 'Cos we wanna go to *Regents*, see…'

'Man, you gotta really *COOL* accent!', the younger woman says, stepping forward. She's audibly chewing gum with open-mouthed enthusiasm and wearing a T-shirt emblazoned with the message: 'OKAY, BUT *WASH* IT FIRST!'

'Get off at *Piccadilly*, it's closer to Regent's street', you say.

'*Piccadilly?* My, ain't that a *darling* name! Piccadilly! Gee, ain't that *cute!*', she says, repeating the word between aggressive mastications.

After serving them, you take another well-earned breather as Eric reopens his window.

'Where do I go for the trains? Up or *down?*' asks the first person.

'Wait at the top of the escalator, mate. The train will come and *pick* you up.' 'There's no need for *sarcasm!*'

'There's *every* need for it!'

'I'll ask you *again*. Where do I go for the *trains?*'

End of the Line

'They call it the underground for a *reason*, mate. Clue's in the *name*', he says, gesturing downwards.

'I see, okay.'

'*Lightbulb* moment for you mate, *yeah?*'

'And how do the gates *open?*'

'Look, Hurry *up* mate, I got half of *Japan* linin' up behind ya! Just ask the bloke on the *barrier*.'

The next passenger asks for a travelcard. 'Five pound *fifty*, is it?', she asks.

'Is this some sort of *game* luv? You guess the fare and I tell you if you're right or *wrong?*'

'Well, how much *is* it?'

'How much is *WHAT?* Come *on* darlin', you're startin' to wear me *DOWN* 'ere!'

'I just want to know what the *fare* is!'

'*What* fare? We'll both be drawing our *pensions* before y'leave this winda if y'don't tell me what y'*want*.'

'I want a *ticket*. Two ways. Is it five pounds *fifty?*'

'A ticket to *where*, love? Is *what* five pounds fifty?'

'I'm going to Finchley Road.'

'*Thass* more like it, love! You could've said that in the *beginnin'!*'

'I did say that in the *beginning!*'

End of the Line

'*Whatever*, love. Customers are always *right* accordin' to them bigwigs up in management.'

The next passenger rocks up. 'Me one day *rover's* not working!' 'That's 'cos you've squished it into a paper *aeroplane*. Look at it, all bent *up.*'

Eric, needing a piss, slaps up a sign which reads 'BACK IN 5 MINS', pulling his blind down on a queue of customers. He just locks his money drawer and potters off. You can hear passengers rapping at the window and calling 'Hello? *Hello?* Anybody there? *Hello?*'

5 minutes later, Eric returns and the window blind shoots up. People are still calling '*Hello? Hello?*' and the man who was originally on the window is still there. 'Where have you bloody *bin* for the last 5 minutes?!' 'Wha-ja *want* me to do, mate, stand here and piss down me *leg?*'

'UP *YOURS*, MATE!'

'AND *YOURS,* with BRASS *BELLS* ON IT!'

Eric turns to you. 'You leave the winda for one minute and there's a fuckin' *'Hello!'*…Or I'll be halfway through makin' a cuppa tea and they'll be a fuckin' *cough!*'

'I'll reopen my window *now*', you suggest, 'to *ease* things.'

'Na! Na! Keep yours *closed,* mate!' He doesn't tell you this for any altruistic reason, it's because a family of lost-looking Americans tourists are approaching and he wants to teach 'them yanks' a lesson. The Americans are wearing T-shirts. The man's T-shirt reads: 'IF YOU THINK EDUCATION IS EXPENSIVE, TRY *IGNORANCE!*' The woman's T-shirt reads: 'THE MEEK SHALL INHERIT *SHIT!*'

Behind them is another woman and an elderly couple. American too, wearing squeaky white sneakers. The couple look like a pair of ancient 5 year olds. The first American smiles at Eric.

'*Gee*, mister, it's one helluva fine *morning!*'

Eric fans a clutch of record cards. 'What's so *good* about it mate?'

'Just wake up and smell the English *tea*, pal!'

Eric de-focuses his eyes, stares ahead into intermediate space. Says nothing.

'Can we git, like, month-long railroad passes for Monday through Friday?'

'You *domiciled* here, sir?'

'We're staying at The Hilton on Park, ain't that *right*, honey?'

The woman, possibly his wife, nods.

'What sort of traveling will you be doing?'

'Of the *subway* variety.'

End of the Line

'Look, mate, let's not play *games*, here. Where do you wanna *go?*'

'Ma-self, Kimberley, ma little pumpkin here, Brooke and the grandparents wanna head on up to the Swiss Chateaux, maybe head on down to Oxford *Circle*.'

'It's a *Circus*.'

'A *circus?*... Hey *honey*, you wanna go see some *trapeze?*'

'Listen, mate! It's a *tube* station, it's called Oxford *Circus*, not *circle*.'

'And where do we find the Swiss *Chateaux* station?'

'Swiss *Cottage*, you mean?'

'Is that name of the *train?*'

'It's the name of the *station*, mate.'

'I see, see, mister, we wanna head up to the GREEN COLLEGE after the Swiss Chateaux. Do we take the *purple* to the *grey?*'

'No, you go from the *blue* to the *silver.*'

'To git ta Green College?...Green-WITCH, I think, ain't that *right*, honey?' he says, consulting with his wife, who's shrugging her shoulders.

End of the Line

'Carry on, mate', Eric says, drumming his fingers.

'Well, see, we wanna head t' REGENT'S *Parkland* and then to tutten–HAIM *court*.'

'Regent's *Park*, mate?'

'Weekly *card?*'

'I said *R-E-G-E-N-T'S P-A-R-K!*'

'Okay, mister. So, do we gotta buy a buncha *tokens?* I guess that's how it works, *huh?* Well, that'll do us mighty *fine*.'

'You're talkin' in *riddles* here mate. What tickets DUE *want* exactly? Are you making statements of *intent*, like, or are you asking me a *question?* We deal in *specifics* here, not *vaguaries*. What tickets d'you *want*, exactly?'

As the American consults his wife, Eric turns towards you with a running commentary. 'These *people!* Bumbling about like Lost fucking *sheep* or forlorn little *lambs*. They know how to travel to the *moon*, but they can't travel 2 stops on the *Underground*. Tube management won't dirty their little shoes dealing with *this* lot! While they're sitting on their sofas in plush offices, ankle-deep in *carpet,* we hafta panda to the great ship of-' Eric stops, stares through the transparent divide as one of the box-card leaflet racks perched on the counter's ledge comes crashing down, feathering leaflets onto the ground. Eric waits a beat.

'You just knocked down me *leaflet* rack, mate! Come

End of the Line

on, exactly what d'you *want* mate? Me psychic guesswork ain't tuned-*up* this mornin'…'

'Oh *Gud*, I CAN'T TAKE THEIR *ACCENTS*, HONEY!' the woman says to her husband, who nods sympathetically.

'Well, I guess we want *six*…'

'SIX *WHAT?* SIX *HAMBURGERS?* SIX PAIRS OF *SHOES?* SIX HOT CROSS *BUNS?* You're makin' hard *work* a this, mate! I'm gettin' the right ol' *HUMP* 'ere!'

'Hey, you need to ease *up* a little, pal. We just want six *tokens*, don't we honey?', the man says, consulting his wife again.

'Pull the other one MATE, it's got *bells* on it! We don't sell *tokens*, here!'

'Well, what in hell's name d'ya *sell* then?'

'We sell *tickets* here, mate! *Tickets!*'

'*TICKETS?* Why, HECK, give us a bunch a *tickets* then! Do we gotta throw 'em into a subway trash barrel at the end of the journey, mister?'

'No. You hold on to 'em tickets mate, *yeah?* Well, we're makin' SOME *PROGRESS* finally 'ere…SO, How many tickets due *want*, exactly?'

'Eight.'

'*EIGHT??* Why don't you get one for the *BUDGIE* as well, mate?'

```
End of the Line
```

The American slides his platinum Ammex *'PREFERRED'* into the change dish, the words *'CURTIS TUTT JNR'* embossed in black against purple.

'Can I *CHARGE* it?'

'You ain't got no *cash* money, no, mate?'

'*No*, mister.'

'You're a *handy* bloke to know, *ain't-cha?*'

The American shrugs, 'Talk about a *BUZZ-KILL!*'

He looks at his wife, who shrugs, 'Beats *me*, Curtis! Lemmee get the billfold outta ya *fanny* pack.'

Curtis unhooks a bundle of greenbacks, unpeels a few from an embossed, shiny silver clip.

'Ya sure ya don't take *plastic*, pal?'

Eric shakes his head, no. He's decided to be difficult.

'Fer *Chrissakes!* Okay, can you at *least* break a *50?*'

'A 50 pound *note?*'

'A 50 *dollar* bill.'

Eric scratches his forehead. The queue has grown 3-fold. 'Is this some kind of candid *camera* thing, mate? Is *Jeremy Beadle* lining up behind ya? We don't take *dollars*. This is *London*, not *L.A.*'

'Wait *up*….' Curtis says, locating some Sterling. 'I

think we're blessed! Are we *blessed*, pal, or do we go to *hell?*' He's smiling now.

Eric takes the money and issues the tickets, his fingers trembling with annoyance. 'Mister, do we shove 'em into the *turnstile?* Do they kick *back?*'

'The gates'll open when they smell your *Paco Rabanne*, mate.'

The American looks at his wife. 'What did he just *say*, honey?'

'Beats *me*, Curtis!'

'I gut one more *question* for ya, mister. My kid here wants to know, why is the *circle line* shaped like a *BOTTLE?*'

'You pullin' me *proverbial?*' Eric screams, cranking down his window blind. It now reads: 'WINDOW POSITION CLOSED'. He's had enough.

'**YOU HAVE A REAL FRIENDLY** *ATTITUDE*, **PAL! GO PISS ON SOME** *OTHER* **TOURISTS,** *FUCKHEAD!*'

End of the Line

CHAPTER EIGHT

The following morning, Big Pete's on the platforms with you.

'Big Pete ta *barrier!*'

'*Pass* it!'

'A lady, dressed in *white*. Head all *red*. Knee-length boots, escalator *three.*'

'Message received!'

'Tell ya what, She can keep them *boots* on!'

'And the *rest!*...good view, yeah?'

'Proper *common*, that one.'

You leave Pete and his wide boy posturing and notice a scrawl on a map. It reads:'Death to AmeriKKKa, the great satan. No compromise with the GAY west!' Beneath it someone's written:'LOVE YOUR *ENEMIES!* LUKE 6:27'.

You carry on walking, past a pictographic decal: A lit cigarette bisected by a red line, replete with leaping, amber flames. You make a few faux checks, checking the platform nosing stones for obstructions, the fire casings for irregularities.

End of the Line

Standing between two adjacent platforms to catch a pleasant crosswind, you notice a movie poster for 'AMERICAN PIE: THE WEDDING'. The strapline reads: 'JIM FINALLY TAKES HER UP THE AISLE'. Someone's crossed out the word *'AISLE'*, replaced it with *'ARSE'*.

Your radio hums. You hold it close to your ear.

'Base to Sidney, come *in!*' SNAP!

'Sidney *receivin'*. Go ahead!' SNAP!

'Did ya get that *ink* cartridge off of that *train*, Sidney?'

'Was it one of them *dynamo* things what *print* things, guv?'

'Yeah, that's *right*, Sidney.'

'Nah, that's a *negative*.'

'Sidders?'

'*Yeah*, guv?'

'If you see the *cleana*...'

End of the Line

'Yeah…?'

'…Tell him the mess-room bog's *blocked* 'an that, yeah?'

'Okee-*cokey*, guv.'

'…And tell Buntiya he needs t'put some water down the ol' *hole*, or summink, *yeah?*'

'Gotcha, guv.'

'Ta!' SNAP!

'Sidney t'base, come *in* base!'

'What is it *now*, Sidney? We just *spoke!*'

'Sidney on the gateline t'base!'

'I just *answered* ya already! What is it *now?*..Message?'

'Sidney t'base. Are you *receivin'*, base?'

'I'll let *you* figure that one out, Sidney…you ought t'get them *ears* washed out.'

'One of them barrier gates is playing *up*, gov…'

'Wos *wrong* wiv it Sidney? Dirty *sensors?*'

'Nah, guv..'

'Dodgey *phota* cell beams?'

End of the Line

'Not *that*, guv…'

'*Diverter* fault?'

'*Nah…*'

'Faulty *contacts?*'

'Don't *fink* so, guv…'

'*What* then?… Loose *paddles?*… *Thermostat* problems?… Trapped *hair?*'

'Not *them*, guv-…'

'Damaged reflectors? *Fluff?*'

'Nah…'

'A power supply surge, or summink, MAYBE?'

'Nah, guv'

'So what's the *problem* then, Sidney?'

'The whatsit's gone tits up.'

'Is that your *technical* assessment, Sidney? The whatsit's gone *TITS UP?*'

'Sidney t'base!'

```
End of the Line
```

'Sid, we're *speakin'* to each other, wos *wrong* with ya?'

'The whatchamacallit's flashin' an' squeekin' like *anyfink*, guv…'

'Are the side paddles *broke*, Sidney?'

'One of 'ems gone or *summink*. It's not powerin' up, over'

'The gate paddles. Are they *broke*, Sidney?'

'They don't seem t'be acceptin' paper tickets no more.'

'Have you checked for any jammed *tickets*, Sidney?'

'Nah, guv.'

'Nah?..Have you fiddled wiv them manual *drive-*knobs?'

'I ain't, *nah*…'

'Sidney, have you checked the *mains* switch?'

'I *thumped* it, guv.'

'*THUMPED* IT?....Sidney…*listen!*…Have you

End of the Line

powered them gates up and down?...This ain't *particle physics*, Sidney...'

'*Nah*, guv..'

'Have you checked the *exit* pods, Sid, or looked for any internal obstructions?'

'I gave the wires a little *tug*.'

'A LITTLE *TUG?!* SIDNEY!, LISTEN!....HAVE YOU NOT HAD NO TECHNICAL TRAINING ON THEM THINGS, *OR WHAT?*'

'Erm...well, guv-'

'-Sounds like it's an *'OR WHAT'*. Now, listen t'me and listen GOOD! Remove the reflector panels and give 'em a GOOD OL' wipe down, *yeah?*'

'*Reflector* panels?'

'Give me flamin' STRENGTH! You ain't one of them *Keystone Kops*, is ya?'

'I can't see no *reflector* panels, guv...'

'Don't y'know what them reflector panels *are*,

End of the Line

Sidders? Please tell me this is a *dream!*'

'Are they like *mirrors?*'

'Fer *fuc*-Okay. FORGET the reflector panels! Have you done a *soft* reset, Sidney?'

'An-*who-?*'

'-A *soft* reset, Sidney!'

'Nah…'

'How about a *hard* reset?'

'Is that the *big* switch on the front?'

'You either HAVE or you AIN'T done a hard reset, Sidney!'

'I ain't done nuffink like *that*, nah, guv…'

'Well, 'ave a little butcher's inside the service panel. Check the SCART LEADS, yeah?'

'I unlocked it but I can't see nuffink except, well… *wires* and *metal*.'

'WIRES AND METAL?…OF COURSE IT'S GOT BLEEDIN' *WIRES* AND *METAL!* IT'S A

End of the Line

FLAMIN' *MACHINE!*....SIDNEY...LOOK...Wos the gate *number?*...YOU UNDERSTAND THE WORD *'NUMBER'*, YEAH?'

'54'

'Is it an *entry* gate?'

'Nah, it *ain't..*'

'Is it an EXIT gate, then?'

'Not one of *those*, nah...'

'Okay, it's not an *exit* OR an *entry* gate?'

'*Nah*, guv...'

'I see....Is it a *bi-directional* gate?'

'Don't *fink* so...'

'Change of wording. Is it a *reversible* gate?'

'Nah...'

'SIMPLE LANGUAGE. Is it a TWO-WAY gate?'

'Yeah, guv. Two-way. It goes *both* ways.'

'*HALLELUYAH!* So it IS a bi-directional then!'

'I DON'T *FINK* SO, guv...'

End of the Line

'*Nice* that!' SNAP!

'*WHAT* IS?' the supervisor asks the unnamed caller. 'Who's *this?*'

'Nice that we're employing people with *Down's Syndrome* now.'

'Leave it *out!* Who *is* this? Mario? *Mario!* LEAVE IT OUT! If Sidney's got *Down's Syndrome*, you've got *Elephantitis!* Sid, this is taking *far* too long. I can't believe the *speed* you guys work! Are you still *there*, Sidney?'

'Er...*yeah*, guv...'

'Lost yer *memory* or sunnink, Sidney?'

'Na, guv...'

'I'll repeat me *question*. In other words, Sidney, is it a *two-way* gate?'

'Er...yeah. *Two* ways, er......'

'You're bein' *ambiguous*, Sidney. What's the two-digit display read?'

'There ain't *no* two-digit display.'

'ARE YOU AN' ME SPEAKIN' THE SAME *LANGUAGE*, SID? Wos the *error* code on the DISPLAY say?'

'*Error* code?'

End of the Line

'Is there a *number*...a little bright pretty red little *number* on the front of the panel?'

'Yeah…'

'OKAY. We're GETTING' somewhere. Wos the *error* fault on it showin'?'

'AY?'

'Has your mind gone A.W.O.L or summink, Sidney?'

'Nah, guv…you want a *number*, yeah?'

'I can't hang about all *day*, I got me phones ringin' all *over* the shop! Come *on* Sidders! I'm waitin' with me *pen* in the air…do's a favour now, yeah? What's the big, red number say?'

'It says…er… 57'.

'*57?*'

'*That's* it, yeah.'

'Looks like we got the *swing* of it now, Sidders, AY?'

'Yeah, guv, *yeah.*'

'OKAY…..LET'S TRY SOME MORE QUESTIONS…..Have you checked the *drive* bands?'

'You talkin' about the *escalator* drive bands?'

End of the Line

'NO YOU *FUC*-the barrier gates 'ere!'

'The gate drive bands, *yeah?*'

'Yeah, y'know, them rubber *pinch* rollers.'

'How do they *look* like, guv?...Sorry, I'm being a bit *slow* this mornin''

'Only this *mornin'?*...Them little black bands inside the gates. Can't miss 'em Sidders, even *YOU* can't miss 'em! They're right *there*, look!'

'Er..hang about, guv...'

'Fanks fer bein' so *proactive*, Sidney.'

'You're *welcome*, guv.'

'*SIDNEY...*'

'Yeah, *GUV?*'

'Sidney, whatja *do* before you come on this job? *BASKET-WEAVING?*'

You notice Pete standing with his radio pressed against his ear. He's giggling silently.

'Can you be a bit more *proactive* next time I ask ya to do summink, Sid? DO WE 'AVE A LITTLE *UNDERSTANDIN'* 'ERE, SIDNEY?'

'Yeah, *righto*. But I fink there's a deffo *defect* on them gates.'

'You, standin' there, *you're* the defect, Sidney!'

End of the Line

'Dya want the *number?*'

'You're beginnin' to *confuse* me now, Sidney. You've already gave me the number, it's 57, *yeah?* Anyway, I won't ask you to check the circuit boards. Just use the pillar switch to let people in and out if it gets busy, *yeah?* Just open up the *manual!*'

'J'want me to fiddle about a bit, gov? See if I can *fix* summink?'

'And your *point* being, Sidney?'

'To bang the problem to *rights*, like gov, over.'

'Listen *careful* to me NOW Sidders! DO NOT *FIDDLE* WITH *NOTHING!* Yeah?'

'Okay guv, but *I-*'

'-*SIDDERS!* GIVE ME A BELL ON THE AUTO! *NOW!*'

You continue walking up and down the platforms and past a McDonalds poster advertising the new 'SALADS PLUS' range. The words 'SALADS PLUS' are printed in big, leafy green letters. Next to the word 'PLUS', someone's added *'FAT'*.

For your meal break today, you take a stroll above ground and head down Oxford street, glancing into the windows of shops. You notice a burly bloke pacing back and forth on a wooden rostrum, mic in hand, barrow boy voice blaring onto the street from an open-fronted fly-by-night store.

End of the Line

'This is the *big* one ladies and gents. This is the one you've all been *waiting* for. 50 bob dresses reduced to £*5!* Money the last thing you *part* with! Come up to the altar and we'll baptize you with a *bargain*, ladies and gents. They say talk's cheap, but money buys the *whiskey!* We have classics, we have separates! We have all the top names! You *know* the names. Let your eyes be the judge! We're a factory outlet selling at factory prices! We got *pinks*, we got *blues*, we got *lilacs*, lavenders, we got *peaches* and *candies*, shell suits for 30 nicker, we even do *nickers*, look.'

You pick up a sandwich and head back to the station, careful not to be late in case Lyndon puts you on extended platform duty, which he does anyway. A little later, you're back on the barriers,

'Classy birds smell of *salmon*…', Pete's saying, leaning against one of the gates, looking over at Sid.

'Yeah…but common birds, like them ones from the Old Kent road 'an that, smell of *kippers*….'

'Them posh birds, mate, they take it up the jacksie. That's *fact*, mate! I ain't being funny or nuffink but the more posh a bird is, the more they're into the ol' *kink* an' that', says Pete.

A woman walks past.

'Look at *that*, look! If ya want a bit a the 'ol tom and dick action, she'd *do* ya, mate!'

'She ain't wearing no *knickers*, look!'

'How can ya *tell?*', Sid asks.

End of the Line

'The 'ol *line* ain't there.'

'Oh, *yeah?* Why don't ya say *'ello* to 'er, mate?'

'I'm a *monogamist*, me. I only *window*-shop. Don't go in an' buy the ol' *goods*. Got me *girlfriend*, see', says Pete.

Big Pete and Sidney now glance over in your direction, at the book you have wedged between the covers of the traffic circular.

'What's all *that* then? *Giz* a look!', Sidney says.

'It's a novel called Candide. It's by *Voltaire*, you explain. Sid and Pete exchange conspiratorial glances and break into hooting laughter. 'You don't half read some *poop*, mate!'

End of the Line

CHAPTER NINE

You're on a platform, walking between the head and tail-wall when you notice a TITANIC THE ARTIFACT exhibition poster. Across it, someone's drawn a stick figure of a waiter wearing a bow tie and holding a tray with a cut glass tumbler on it. A speech-bubble protruding from the waiter's mouth, asks:

'BLOCK OF *ICEBERG* IN YOUR G & T, SIR?'

Your radio rattles. 'Base t'Charlie-Tango-9!'

'Pass you message, base…', you say through a shudder of interference.

'State yer current *location*, over!'

'Platform 2, approaching the tail-wall, over.'

'We needja to man the gate-line, *over!*'

'Rodger that.'

You head to the gate-line.

'Alright?' You say to your colleagues as you approach.

'*Alight?*' One of them replies.

You notice a TWIRLY. OAPs on the tube are known as 'TWIRLIES'. Their freedom passes only work from 9am, but more often than not, they rock up earlier. The OAP's tapping her freedom pass against a gate reader, but it's not activating, it keeps bleeping in objection. You approach.

'Am I *TWIRLY?*'

'You are a bit *early*, yes. 5 minutes too early', you say.

'Five *minutes*, officer?'

'It gets activated at 9.'

'So, I have to wait five minutes, 'til *9?*'

'It's 8.55 now.'

'It only works at *9*, officer?'

'It does. 5 minutes.'

'5 *minutes?* I need to wait *five* minutes?'

Meanwhile, a tramp steals through the luggage flap on his hands and knees as another passenger vaults the gates. You feel a tap you on the shoulder, you turn round.

'You gotta let me *girlfriend* froo mate, else I won't get a *bunk-up* tonight', the man says with a wink. You release the courtesy gate and let his girlfriend through. 'It's *Belinda!*' he whispers conspiratorially.

An uneventful hour passes until a crusty steps off the cowl of the escalator whistling a come command at a dog. It all happens very quickly. There's a black blur, a hysterical yap and a drawn-out, lachrymose howl followed by a surge of maroon. A Rottweiler with a red bandana tied round its neck is thrashing around violently, spurting blood, its paw trapped in the escalator treads.

End of the Line

Pete throws his jacket over the dog's mahogany head and hits the emergency stop as Lyndon rushes over, huffing and puffing, having put a call through to the controller.

'Vet's on the *way*', he announces. 'Just been on the blower to the *ol' man.*'

'Dogs ain't *allowed* up them escalators!' Lyndon's haranguing the crusty as the dog snaps and growls, its paws ribboned with blood.

'My *poor* Fifi!'

Mario, a colleague with a carbuncled face and greasy hair, barriers the escalator off as Lyndon heads to the machine chamber to trip the circuit breakers. When he returns, he stands for a moment with a comb-lifting tool in one hand, wondering how to lift the offending section of tread without being flayed to ribbons.

Luckily, the vet appears, wearing a lab coat and brandishing a bag. Crouching down, he opens his bag, secretes an arm into one of the compartments and removes an air rifle. Resting on his knees now, he attaches the trigger of the rifle to its barrel, screws on a dart, unscrews two bottles of sedative and transfers the contents into the barrel of a syringe.

You keep the passengers behind a safety cordon as the vet readies himself with a PERMA GAS canister. In a series of sibilant hisses, he gasses the dart, attaches a fly-feather to its rear, fits the dart to

End of the Line

the gun and, using a foot-pump attached to the gun cylinder, pumps it hard with his shoe. Stepping gingerly towards the cowl with his rifle at the ready, he takes careful aim and shoots at the dog's hindquarters. Within seconds, the creature falls forward with an audible thud. The vet rushes forward and fits the dog with a muzzle, looping it across its head as three barrier staff scramble to shift the dog clear of the escalator.

The pad of one paw has been torn so badly its now a miasma of hanging flesh, leaving a spattered line of blood running from the escalator to the dog's flayed pad. Lyndon drops to his knees, removes the cover plate on the step riser with his comb-lifting tool and hangs an OUT OF SERVICE sign from its side panel.

The vet dabs the dog's wound with cotton wool dampened with some sort of sterilising solution, then applies a conforming bandage, leaving cotton balls lodged between its paws. He's now wrapping a dressing to seal the bandage in place, a dressing decorated with a repeating pattern of paw prints and the word *'OUCH!'*

The vet injects the Rottie with a pain killer from a needle-tipped syringe and administers a secondary injection to reverse the sedation. Soon the dog stirs, attempts to stand on unsteady paws but staggering and dazed, drops to its haunches, its black lips quivering.

'Hello there, I'm *Danny*, what's your name?', the vet says to the crusty, with you at her side.

End of the Line

'It's *Mandy*.' She's visibly shaken.

The vet explains that the dog has sustained a degloving injury and suggests intravenous antibiotics and regular bandage changes.

'Normally, Mandy, I'd've clipped hair from the dog's foreleg and injected its cephalic vein, but given the situation, I had no alternative, I *hope* you understand.'

'Will Fifi *recover?*'

'The pads grow back. Change Fifi's dressings every day, wet to dry and use a K-band dressing, *with* me? It's a pretty *hardy* breed, the Rottie. Your beloved Fifi will be *okay*.'

Lyndon summons the crusty into the ops room with you as her escort.

'Take a *pew*' he tells the crusty, with you standing behind her.

'Do I need to fill in any *forms?*' the crusty asks, looking around.

'Do you know *why* I've asked ya in here, luv?'

'To fill in some forms, *no?*'

'*Why*. That's the question I wanna ask ya, luv. *Why?*'

'Why *what?*'

'Well, for starters, why was y'dog *unleashed?*'

End of the Line

'I've *gotta* leash', the crusty says, motioning to a length of old rope.

'Never noticed them *signs,* love? Dogs on escalators have to be *carried.*'

'*Carried?* Look at the bleedin' *size* of her! She weighs soddin' 40 *pounds!*'

'That's how come y'hafta use the fixed *stairway*, love, or inform a member of staff so as we can halt them escalators. You've gave me a right ol' headache now, them escalators can't be put back in service 'til the engineers give 'em the once over. Yer gonna fill some incident forms now, *yeah?*'

As you leave, you notice some kids stroking the dog. It's lying on the ground, muzzled, half dazed, waiting for its owner with bloodshot, rheumy eyes and a large sliver of saliva on its ruff.

CHAPTER TEN

You're looking at the posters along the platform walls. One reads:A Flora Aerobathon: The world's largest ever aerobics workout. An image depicts several sweat-soaked women in leotards. Next to the word Aerobathon, is a sticker which reads: This *denigrates* women. Across the sticker someone's scribbled: 'Yeah, but *Mario* likes it!'

After your shift, you head home and hit the sack. Once you drop into the arms of Morpheus, you have a dream that you're making your way towards Kings cross station, scuttling past the BR wheelchair ramps and fast-food stalls to board a northbound GNER train bound for Darlington, where you have to change for the shuttle service to Grimsby. You're trying to get as far away from the tube as you can.

You're now on the shuttle-service as it chatters past East Didsbury, Stockport, Scunthorpe and Grimsby Town. As you alight at the yellow buffers, you see a woman. She's standing and waving at you.

She leads you to a shop filled with crystal-cast animal figurines of bullfrogs, moorland sheep, flopsy rabbits, hound pups, a female Charlie Chaplin with porn-star breasts, a dog sitting in giant shoes, flocked rabbits, salt-pot pigs, grinning Alligators and a bearded Collie fashioned from porcelain. The woman says her name's Liberty and she leads you outside, her arm looped in yours.

You pass a woman holding a bunch of foil-wrapped

End of the Line

heather. She looks vaguely familiar. She's looks into your eyes. 'Remember *me?*', she says. 'Oh, I think you *do* remember me. You *refused* to buy me lucky heather. *Bad luck* not to buy heather from a traveller, me darlin'' she says, breaking into a rising, rolling, ululating cackle.

Up ahead a kid with a red bucket and a green scooter skips beside his mum who's pushing a large, polka-dotted pram. Behind the woman and her boy is a black Rottie which starts to jump at the woman's shoulders. You notice it has a limp. The woman's wearing a necklace with the name SANDRA on it and she's screaming at the dog to get down.

'Gerroff me you mardi-assed *sod!*', she screams, 'Pack it *in* you little ratter! Oo joo think you *are*, the queen *mother?* Goo on! Joomp off, you stoopid lummox! You're worse than the *kids,* you are. Now get down and give *over!*' Nearby, an elderly woman on a wooden bench sits with her bloomers flapping in the wind. You try to stroke Liberty's hair.

'No pet!...We're not doin' none of *that!*'

The two of you are now walking towards the sandy beach. There are penny arcades lining the shore and a rail track running off to the side attached to wooden sleepers, but it's the *end of the line*. The track terminates at a building raked with light. In front of the building, Lyndon's standing, his forehead furrowed, his arms akimbo. He's wearing swimming trunks and a peaked cap.

'What was it *today?*', he says, not even deigning to

look up. 'Leaves on the *track?*'

THE END

Printed in Great Britain
by Amazon